# ALI SPARKES
# MONSTER MAKERS

Ready to rock!

# Rockataur

Illustrated by Dynamo Ltd

**■ SCHOLASTIC**

*To Jacob and Alex, creators of Taurs*

*Thanks to Emily Anderson for creating Tryangletaur*

First published in the UK in 2009 by Scholastic Children's Books
An imprint of Scholastic Ltd
Euston House, 24 Eversholt Street
London, NW1 1DB, UK
Registered office: Westfield Road, Southam, Warwickshire, CV47 0RA
SCHOLASTIC and associated logos are trademarks and
or registered trademarks of Scholastic Inc.

Text copyright © Ali Sparkes, 2009
Illustration copyright © Dynamo Design, 2009

The right of Ali Sparkes and Dynamo Design to be identified as the author
and illustrator of this work has been asserted by them.

Cover illustration © Dynamo Design, 2009

ISBN 978 1 407 10872 8

A CIP catalogue record for this book is available
from the British Library

Printed by CPI Bookmarque, Croydon, CR0 4TD
Papers used by Scholastic Children's Books are made from wood
grown in sustainable forests.

1 3 5 7 9 10 8 6 4 2

www.scholastic.co.uk/zone

## Chapter One

# Blunder on the Battlements

The turret of the castle loomed high, grey and menacing. Arrows shot from the narrow archers' windows in its stone tower, bringing sudden death to anyone trying to attack from below without a shield. An army was besieging the stronghold; a crowd of round-headed soldiers in square red tunics, poised for the bloodiest battle imaginable.

On top of the turret, surrounded by low walls, a red flag rippling in the breeze above their heads, Jack and Lewis were locked in mortal combat. Their swords clashed and rang as they fought inside the circle of stone. Jack was taller and more expert at fencing, but Lewis was fast and deadly. As Jack swung around the

1

flagpole, his sword cutting a lethal arc through the air, Lewis darted under his shield, stabbed his foot and pushed him off the tower.

"AAAAAAARRRRRRGGGGGHHHH!" screamed Jack as he plummeted to certain death. To think . . . his *own brother* had slain him. . .

"Are you dead?" cackled Lewis. "Are you splattered all over the drawbridge? Yay! I rock!"

"I'm not . . . quite . . . dead . . . yet. . ." wheezed Jack.

"You are! You're snapped in half. Your legs have come off!"

"No, they're still attached – see!" Jack put his legs back on with a small click but Lewis wasn't having any of it.

"You're dead and you know it! I've won."

"Ah, but. . ." Jack thought fast, resurrecting his body and defiantly lifting his sword. "I am coming back as a ghost . . . even stronger!"

"Rubbish! That's cheating." Lewis leaned over and flicked his brother's reassembled body into the crowd of soldiers. A small green figure and a taller blue one toppled over as it struck

2

them. "And *what* are Yoda and Doctor Who doing in your army?" demanded Lewis. "It's Lego soldiers *only*. You can't go chucking in a Jedi and a Time Lord. That's not fair."

"Yeah it is," muttered Jack, retrieving his soldier figure and reattaching its legs once again. "Yoda was bored with fighting the Empire and fancied helping out – and the Doctor just stumbled in from a different space-time continuum. I can't help *that*."

"Boys! Are you ready to go?" Mum called up from downstairs, and Jack and Lewis abandoned their small plastic siege and hurtled downstairs. Normally they went to visit their Aunt Thea on a Saturday and they would complain bitterly if they couldn't. At Aunt Thea's they could magic their monster friends – Electrotaur and Slashermite – up from the underground world of Tauronia. Electrotaur and Slashermite were *real* monsters, who had been drawn by Jack and Lewis and then brought to life with magic Merrion's Mead. They were safely kept away from the real world with many other Taurs and Mites (also drawn and meaded to life by Jack

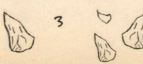

3

and Lewis) – but they could come up to play in Aunt Thea's back garden, through the standing stone which also served as the Gateway to Tauronia.

Normally Jack and Lewis wouldn't miss playing with Electrotaur and Slashermite (who looked as scary as they sounded, but were quite friendly) for anything. But today, Mum and Dad were taking them on a trip to a *real* castle. Their wooden swords were tucked into their belts. Soon they would be able to get locked in mortal combat on an *actual* turret. They couldn't *wait*.

"Oh why do we have to *wait?*" wailed Lewis, slumping against the stone wall. The queue to get in seemed to stretch for ever. It was a rare sunny Saturday in late September and every family in the county seemed to have had the same idea. Trindle Castle lay ahead of them, clinging to the side of a small hill, all grey rock and towers and crenellated walls. ("Crenellated," Jack had discovered from the leaflet on the way in the car, "means the rock

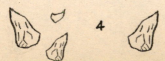

brick bits which go up and down, you know, like our Lego bricks, on the top of the castle.") It looked fantastic, even though it was quite a small castle. It had a moat with water in it, and a drawbridge.

"It's got a portcullis!" said Jack, peering past the people in front of them in the queue. "You know, the criss-cross metal gate with spikes on the bottom, that they used to drop on to invaders."

"I *know* what a portcullis is!" snapped Lewis. "I am nearly *eight* you know!"

"So . . . who lived in the castle?" wondered Jack, flicking the leaflet over for some clue.

A little girl in front of them turned around and fixed them with her round brown eyes. "A pwincess, of course!" she said. She held out her Princess Flowerdew dolly and both Jack and Lewis flinched backwards. They'd had issues with Princess Flowerdew in the past, that were best not spoken of.

"Pwincesses live in castles," continued their small pink-cardiganed adviser. "That's what castles are *for.*"

"Nah," said Lewis. "Castles aren't for

princesses to live in. They're just great big rock and metal killing machines! See – little windows for arrows to come out of, spikes on the portcullis to skewer enemies, gaps in the gateway for pouring boiling oil on people, the moat for drowning people, dungeons for torture." He beamed happily as the round brown eyes got rounder. "But yeah, sometimes they put princesses in the towers. Or sometimes the dungeons. They'd go to dances and banquets and stuff – and then they'd get their heads chopped off by the king."

The little girl's lower lip began to tremble and Jack elbowed Lewis in the ribs.

"They do *not* get their heads chopped off by the king!" protested the little girl, but she turned away from them and stared at Princess Flowerdew for a moment before tugging hard on the doll's blonde ringlets with horrified wonder. Princess Flowerdew's head only resisted a few seconds before there was a small *pop* and it came off, still smiling eerily. Then the crying started.

"Oh well done, Lew!" Jack whacked the

6

back of his brother's head.

"It wasn't my fault! I didn't *ask* her to decapitate her doll, did I?"

Once they all got inside the castle, it was great. While Mum and Dad followed the guide around and nodded with interest at the old fireplaces and stone carvings, Jack and Lewis used the castle for what it was actually *meant* for. Fighting.

It was mostly ruined anyway, apart from some rooms in one wing which were still used by the castle owners, apparently, and the guided tour area. Jack and Lewis ran through the tour rooms with proper floors and windows and old paintings and stuff to look at, but the ruined bits were better. There were spiral stone steps leading up to the towers and little alcoves with narrow archers' windows where you could pretend to shoot out arrows at enemies.

"Look, it's a garderobe! This is their toilet!" marvelled Jack, pausing at a small stone room off the spiral staircase they were climbing. It was just big enough to sit in, with a stone slab resting at seat height. In the slab was a round hole. Jack peered into it and saw nothing but blackness.

"The poo used to fall on people's heads below!" Lewis gurgled with mirth. "Aunt Thea told me about that. She said it was a lot like going to Glastonbury Festival."

"No, it used to go into the moat," said Jack, peering out through the tiny window in the toilet room.

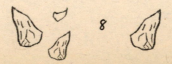

"You're quite right, young man," said a friendly voice and Jack and Lewis glanced around in surprise to see a lady, wearing a red Trindle Castle blazer, peering through the doorway at them. She had curly grey hair and there was a badge on a ribbon around her neck, which read: Marjorie – Friend of Trindle Castle. She must be one of the volunteer guides, thought Jack.

"The poo *did* used to fall into the moat – to make it all the nastier for anyone thinking about swimming across and scaling the walls! Imagine the smell on a hot day. Phew! *This* was a luxury toilet, mind you, for the lord and lady of the castle. There were a few more for very special guests, but all the soldiers and the lowly people who *worked* here would have had to make do with a bucket or a pot, kept under their bed. It was some poor soul's work to collect them all up and empty them over the battlements into the moat. Imagine! A poo monitor. Bet you wouldn't fancy a job like *that* much!"

"Eeeuuw!" gurgled Lewis, hugely entertained.

"It's a fabulous place, isn't it?" said the

lady, moving back on to the steps and sighing happily. "I used to run up and down these steps pretending to be a knight when I was your age. Ah, if only these walls could talk! It's wonderful that it's getting properly restored at last. They're even carting all the big boulders up from the hill where they fell years and years ago, and rebuilding parts of the building – just like an old jigsaw."

"Yes, it's brilliant," said Jack, with a polite smile, remembering the piles of grey rock they'd seen just outside the castle walls as they were queuing to get in. Marjory, Friend of Trindle Castle, smiled back and carried on down the staircase.

"Come on!" yelled Lewis, charging on up the steps, which rose in a right-handed spiral. He turned backwards, his sword drawn, ready to battle Jack all the way.

Jack followed, hanging awkwardly on to the rope which was looped through old iron rings on the outer wall, clacking his own sword viciously against Lewis's as they went – until his younger brother turned and ran up and out of

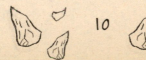

sight, whooping with excitement. Jack slowed down and looked around him, trying to imagine what this had been like four hundred years ago, when people really lived here. The steps were steep and had been worn down into smooth shiny dips in the middle. The stone smelled old and cold. Thick spider webs softened the corners of every window he passed.

"Aaaw!" Up at the top, Lewis was staring at the bit of turret he wanted to get to next, further along the stone ramparts that ran around the inner keep. There was a bright orange rope knotted across the stone archway with a sign hanging from it which read: *No public access. Restoration work in progress.*

"That's the *best* turret!" whined Lewis, slumping down, cross-legged on to the floor. "I want to go in *that* one!"

"Well, we can't," said Jack, sitting down next to him and opening the guidebook which Mum had bought for them. "It's not going to be finished until. . ." he looked at the map of the castle and read the bit about the ongoing work to rebuild parts of it, ". . .next March."

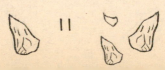

"Bum," muttered Lewis. He went to look over the thick stone wall, into the inner courtyard below. There were loads of people roaming around, looking down the castle well and trailing in and out of the gift shop, but nobody else up on the top bit with them right now. "We should make our *own* castle with magic mead! Then we could live in it – and have battles whenever we liked. We could put it in the woods by Aunt Thea's house, where nobody would see it."

"Of course they'd see it," said Jack, fishing his glasses out of his pocket so he could read better. "We're not the only people who ever go in the woods. And anyway, you know the rule. We can't use Merrion's Mead for anything in the real world. We can only use it to make our monsters come alive in Tauronia."

"I don't see why," sulked Lewis.

"So having your drawing of a mad flower-shaped assassin wandering around and nearly killing school bullies was OK, was it?"

"Baz was all right after the antidote," argued Lewis.

12

"And having a nine-year-old criminal mastermind brainwash our school and nearly take over the world with Merrion's Mead was all fine by you, was it?"

"Well... Hey – I know! We could bring Slashermite up to live in the castle and he could just hypnotize anyone who ever saw it, so they wouldn't remember!" Lewis was very proud of Slashermite's special talent for hypnotism. It had come in very handy in a number of adventures.

"We're lucky Aunt Thea hasn't tipped the whole lot down the sink by now," said Jack. "Especially after all those Taurs and Mites showed up in her garden last month. We only sent Ninjataur back to Tauronia half a second before Mum saw him!"

"Aunt Thea would never tip our mead away," said Lewis. "She loves Electrotaur and Slashermite and Tauronia as much as we do."

Jack thought Lewis was probably right. And after all, it was Aunt Thea who had started the whole amazing business in the first place. She had found the bottles of Merrion's Mead in a little shop somewhere in the Welsh

Valleys and heard about the legend that it was able to bring dreams to life. She thought the boys would think it was funny to have a bottle each.

Of course, none of them actually *believed* the legend. Not until Jack and Lewis accidentally spilled the mead on their drawings of mad monsters – and had then woken up a few hours later to find Electrotaur, an eight foot buzzing electricity beast, and Slashermite, a small purple blade-fingered monster with a rhino horn, alive in their bedroom.

After *that* adventure Jack and Lewis had needed somewhere safe for their creations to live, so they had drawn Tauronia – a mad, wonderful and dangerous land. But although they could get their safer monsters up to play from time to time, they were forbidden to go down to Tauronia. It was just too likely to end in death.

"Maybe we could make a castle, just for us, in Tauronia," Lewis was saying now. "I mean, we've already made one for Electrotaur and Slashermite to live in down there, and loads of

others for other Mites and Taurs. So why not one for us?"

"Because we're not allowed into Tauronia, remember? We promised Aunt Thea."

"We've been anyway. Twice."

"Yes, but those were emergencies."

"Suppose we created a special safe zone for just us and our castle?"

"She'll never let us," said Jack. "Remember when we nearly got eaten by Grippakillataur?"

There was a knocking noise on the far side of the stone doorway which was roped off. Someone was obviously at work there right now, restoring the castle.

"Shut up about it, anyway," said Jack. "People might hear you!"

Lewis shrugged and got up to go back down the spiral stone steps. "Who cares? Nobody ever believes us." He spotted a couple of workmen in overalls on the far side of the stone archway and another man in a grey suit. All were wearing yellow hard hats. "We make monsters with magic!" he shouted. Only the man in the suit looked up. He stared at Lewis for a moment before dropping his eyes back down to a clipboard and turning to the men in overalls.

"Real live ones!" sang out Lewis. "Made real with magic Merrion's Mead. Our Aunt Thea brought it back from Wales and we've been making monsters come to life ever since!"

Jack shoved him towards the steps. "Stop being a noobstick!" he hissed, although he knew Lewis was right. Nobody ever *believed* their stories about Tauronia. Nobody had a clue what Merrion's Mead could do.

As they went down the stairs, Jack didn't notice the man in the suit step through the stone archway and stare down after them, his small eyes glittering and his fleshy face turning pink.

One of the workmen arrived behind him. "Oh, by the way, sir – about the carving above the door. . . Sir? Are you all right?"

The man in the suit turned to him, running his hand through his thinning dark hair and gnawing at his lower lip. He didn't seem to be *seeing* his employee at all.

16

The workman gulped and stepped back. "Erm. . . Do you need to sit down? Sir? Lord Merrion?"

## Chapter 2

# AWOL in the Overworld

*"Ninja . . . Ninja . . . Ninjataur. . ."* Aunt Thea's voice rang softly and musically through the trees. A little way off, along the river, Jack and Lewis were also calling out in a whisper. It was absurd. They needed to shout – but they didn't dare to. She looked around anxiously. She didn't want any passing neighbour to think she'd gone mad, (or madder) and she also didn't want to risk frightening Ninjataur away. Which was ridiculous in itself. A near-invisible creature which could move at the speed of lightning and camouflage itself against any backdrop was not likely to be afraid of *her*.

Jack and Lewis trooped over to join her, looking very guilty – as well they might! They'd

been dropped over to her house for tea after the day at Trindle Castle and at first everything was fine. They had brought their aunt a gift from the castle – a lacy handkerchief which had *Trindle Castle* embroidered in one corner with purple silk thread. She'd been very pleased and immediately tucked it into the pocket of her grey cashmere waistcoat. Then everything had become less than fine – a lot less.

Jack and Lewis had begged to get Ninjataur up to do sword fighting with them. With his ninjato – a Japanese short sword which Lewis had designed very carefully before meading – he was the obvious choice to join in with their game.

But Ninjataur had a recent history of disappearing. He'd been AWOL (absent without leave) for more than twenty-four hours last time and heaven only knew how close Aunt Thea's neighbours had come to having their throats cut. So, obviously, she had said no.

And then *one* of her nephews had "*accidentally*" meaded Ninjataur up anyway. She'd found them all, having a fierce mock battle around the back of the standing stone, and shouted, "Jack! Lewis! What on earth?!" Half a second later Ninjataur had shot down her garden, up over her roof and off into the woods in a blur of blue silk. By the time they'd all hurtled out of the front door he was nowhere to be seen.

A flicker of movement off to the right had Aunt Thea spinning on her heel and staring up into the branches. "Shh!" she said, beckoning Jack and Lewis closer and pointing up into the trees. "Look, there he is!" Ninjataur sat casually in an oak tree, his back resting against the thick trunk and one leg along a branch; the other swinging from it. He regarded them with glittery silver eyes, through the narrow slit in his navy blue hood thing. He was covered from his horned head to his pointed toes in swathes of blue silk, with only a narrow gap for him to see through. He moved like an assassin and carried his ninja sword in a dark-blue silk belt.

"Ninjataur!" scolded Lewis. "You're not allowed to go off on your own in the Overworld! We've spent the last twenty minutes looking for you!"

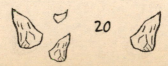

He scribbled "Ninjataur gows home imedietly" in his usual dodgy spelling, while Aunt Thea got out one of their little wooden bottles of Merrion's Mead. They could have done this at the cottage, of course, but Ninjataur was so fast and so shadowy that he might have gone in any direction and Lewis needed to have some idea of where he was to be able to send him back. It was the same with creating monsters – the boys needed to visualize where they would appear.

"Right, off you go home now," said Lewis, letting a few drops of mead drip across his drawing. Ninjataur folded his arms and moodily stared down at them, but a few seconds later there was a popping noise and the oak branch was empty.

They all sighed with relief.

"You two," growled Aunt Thea as she stomped back through the trees, the soggy earth ruining her favourite green leather boots, "are in a lot of trouble! If your mum and dad hadn't gone away for the night I would be sending you straight home. Don't think you'll be getting any

21

hot chocolate and biscuits before bedtime!"

Jack and Lewis looked at each other bleakly. They knew they'd been bad. It was the excitement of the castle and playing at being knights which had made them do such a stupid thing. They said nothing and as soon as they got back to the house they began to silently tidy all the Tauronia drawings back into the special folder which went into the drawer in the big pine kitchen table. Lewis put the crayons back in their jar and Jack handed Aunt Thea the half-empty bottle of mead, which she put up into the high cupboard where another three full bottles were kept.

"Right, now you can go and collect your swords from behind the standing stone," said Aunt Thea. Jack and Lewis nodded and trudged out to the garden, closing the kitchen door behind them.

"You shouldn't have done it, Lew!" muttered Jack, as they reached the column of serpentine rock which stood tall but slightly bent, like a giant finger beckoning at the heavens.

"You shouldn't have let me," said Lewis.

Jack opened his mouth but then closed it again. Lewis was right – he *shouldn't* have let him. But they'd only meant to have a very, very quick, *little* sword fight and then send Ninjataur right back down into Tauronia. The door to the monsters' world was now closed and the standing stone looked ordinary enough as they went behind it to pick up their swords. They didn't hurry. They weren't keen to go back into the house when Aunt Thea was so cross with them.

"She really might pour the mead down the sink this time," murmured Jack.

Lewis said nothing. He knew it was his fault really. He leaned against the red and black speckled rock and stared dismally at his feet.

"Come on, we need to go and say sorry. Properly," said Jack.

They went back down the garden and opened the door to the kitchen. Aunt Thea wasn't in it. The high cupboard door was open and no twiggy bottles of mead were to be seen.

"Oh no!" cried Lewis. "She's pouring it down the toilet or something!"

They raced upstairs to the bathroom, but

Aunt Thea wasn't there either. Then back down to the front garden, in case she was pouring the mead directly into the drain. Nobody was in the front garden.

Jack and Lewis looked at each other, gulping.

"Maybe she walked up the shop," said Lewis. "Her car's still here."

"Without telling us?" said Jack. He suddenly felt his skin prickle with a very bad feeling as they went back into the cottage. "Lew . . . something is wrong."

"I know," said Lew.

They ran up and down the stairs again and all around the garden, then up and down the road.

Aunt Thea was gone. The mead was gone.

"Jack! Look!" Lewis ran towards something white and fluttering in the road. As he caught up with his brother, Jack bit his lip. Lying on the tarmac, a little way along the road from Aunt Thea's cottage, was the lacy Trindle Castle handkerchief. An oily tyre track ran across it.

Jack picked it up and they both stared along the road. There were no cars racing away –

everything was quiet. No neighbours were out cutting hedges or walking back from the shops.

They went back into the house. They stood in the kitchen, staring from the handkerchief to the empty cupboard and then at each other.

"Has someone kidnapped her?" whispered Lewis, his eyes big with fear.

Jack wanted to say that was a silly idea – but he was thinking the same thing. Surely nobody would have kidnapped Aunt Thea. It just couldn't be. No.

"Yeeeezzzz," said a voice above them.

Jack and Lewis jumped and stared up in shock. Hanging upside down from the light fitting was Ninjataur.

"Men come," he said, in a strange, high voice, his words billowing through his silken mask.

"She and leetle boddles . . . men tek zem all. . ."

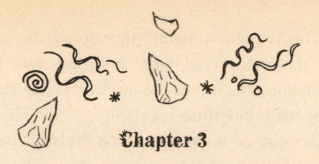

# Chapter 3

# Loathsome Lording and Dodgy Dialogue

"You'll never get away with this, you know," said Aunt Thea. She cringed. With embarrassment. She sounded like someone in a cheesy mystery cartoon.

"Oh, I think I will," chuckled the man with the sweaty red face. He had obviously decided he was in a cheesy mystery cartoon too and was joining in with the bad dialogue. "It's no use trying to get away. You can't escape. *I have the power now!*"

"You're nothing more than a common thief," retorted Aunt Thea. She sighed and gave a shrug. It was another dreadful line, but right now she couldn't come up with anything better.

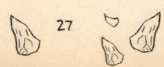

"This is my *birthright!*" thundered the man with the sweaty red face, towering over her and shaking his fist in the air. Except his voice wasn't really like thunder, thought Aunt Thea – it was more of a whine, with a Welsh accent. And he only towered over her because she was tied to a chair and he was standing on a box. And he was only shaking his fist because there was a spider on it. Now he flicked it off with a little shudder, and then began to rub his hands together, staring at her with great intensity.

All in all, her captor was a bit lame, reflected Aunt Thea. He was rubbing his hands together because she'd bitten them during the struggle as he and two other men had bundled her down her hallway and he was now working some Savlon into the puncture wounds. Aunt Thea had rather sharp canines.

"Aaah," he said. "That's better. Now!" He checked the rope that bound her to the chair. "Do as you're told and you won't get hurt. But if you try anything funny—"

"What – like a comedy routine?" said Aunt Thea. It was hard to take her captor seriously.

Even the two blokes in workmen's overalls had to bite their lips behind the sweaty red-faced man's back. "Can't do stand-up. I'm tied to a chair."

"Don't you mess with me!" he warned.

"Would like to. But must refer you to my earlier comment about being tied to a chair."

"Why, you. . ." He held his fist up, threateningly. "You seem to forget, Miss Casterbridge, who has the upper hand here."

"No, I can see quite clearly that *you* have," said Aunt Thea with a tight smile. "Is it all still hurty? Did I mention that I am a carrier of rabies?"

"GAG HER!" thundered the man. And this time he really did thunder. Aunt Thea nodded wearily. She tended to have this effect on men, even when she wasn't being held prisoner in a stone dungeon, tied to a chair.

"But wait," she said, as the two men in boiler suits advanced with a manky-looking bit of tea-towel. "Aren't you going to tell me about your dastardly plan?"

The man waved off his henchmen and stared

at her for a moment.

"Perhaps you ought to know. After all, you'll never get a chance to tell anyone. And nor will your nephews once I've found them!"

Aunt Thea gulped. He knew about Jack and Lewis? She tried not to look panicked.

She'd been annoyed when she'd first been kidnapped. Yes. Really quite cross. But on her travels around the world she had got out of trickier situations with more dangerous men than *this*. Warring terrorists in Afghanistan, Mafia thugs in Sicily, double glazing salesmen in Swindon. Sadly, though, she *knew* that her captor had all the Merrion's Mead and seemed to understand what it could do. If he could make it work it would be very easy for him to get rid of her. But the only thing that really scared her was what might happen to poor Jack and Lewis. By sheer good fortune they had been out of sight, at the top of the garden, when the three men had arrived on her doorstep.

When she'd been frogmarched back to her kitchen, they had known exactly what to look for and her dratted high cupboard door

hadn't been shut. The sweaty pink-faced one recognized the bottles in it immediately. They'd counted them all up, including the empties, and popped them into a little cardboard box.

She'd had no choice but to give them up and then go quietly with them. She couldn't manage a hand-to-hand combat situation with three men. Two, maybe – one, definitely. But three was too many. And she had been terrified that Jack and Lewis would come back in at any moment, and get caught up in the robbery. The only thing she could think of doing as she was hustled quickly out to a big white delivery van and shoved inside, was to drop her lovely new handkerchief, in the hope that Jack or Lewis would see it and realize she'd been taken somewhere against her will. A forlorn plan – and what could they do, anyway? She didn't want them to risk a rescue. She wanted to get out of this by herself.

The sweaty pink-faced man was building up to revealing his dastardly plan. "My name," he said, pulling himself up tall and inflating his podgy chest, "is Lord Alun Byron Daffyd Merrion."

"*Oh*," said Aunt Thea. She *was* surprised.

"I am the great great great great *great* grandson of the fabled Lord Merrion for whom Merrion's Mead was created."

"Now look, be realistic . . . you're not *that* great," said Aunt Thea, firmly but kindly. "Silence!" he bellowed, showering her left arm with little flecks of spit. "You must see, madam, that *I* am the rightful heir to any Merrion's Mead still existing today!"

"It's 'miss', actually," said Aunt Thea. "And I agree nothing. I bought those bottles of mead, fair and square, from a shop in Llantribble. There was no notice up about them belonging to anyone else. So I think you can let me go and take this up with the shopkeeper."

"The shopkeeper," hissed Lord Merrion, leaning nastily close to her so she could see the gooey white spit which had built up in the corners of his mouth, "has shut up shop and left the country!"

"So, how did you trace the mead to me?" asked Aunt Thea, actually genuinely interested – in spite of her worries.

"I have spent many years searching for the truth of the mead," declared Lord Merrion, suddenly standing upright and then beginning to pace theatrically up and down. "For centuries the story of its power to bring the stuff of dreams to life has been handed down through generations of Merrions. Of course, many believe it is just a fairy story, but not I, no – not I! I have always known it was *real*! I *had* to find it!" He pounded his right fist into his left palm to make his point and then whimpered as the puncture wounds from Aunt Thea's teeth smarted.

"In recent years," he went on, after a deep

33

breath, "I had almost given up. Leaving our ancestral home in Wales, I instead focused my considerable talents on rebuilding the spare family castle at Trindle, in readiness for a new money-making venture." He turned to Aunt Thea, his small eyes glittering with glee. "It's going to be just like Alton Towers, right? Only better because it's got history in it too! Loads of rides and stuff, like rollercoasters, right? All swooping past the castle walls and towers and a high speed historical commentary as people go past, screaming! Like . . . *thisiswhereJamesthethirdtookaholiday* . . . AAAAAAAAAAAAAAAAH . . . and now *"AnneBoleynstayedhere"* . . . AAAAAAAAAAH! Yes! I will call it the Shrieking History Rollercoaster, or the Hysterical Historical! Yes . . . I like that."

He paused, panting, for a few seconds.

"You might want to note that there *was* no James the third," suggested Aunt Thea.

"So, anyway," went on Lord Merrion. "I was planning my fantastic new Trindle Castle Theme Park, up with the workmen on the

northern battlement, when I happened to hear two children. Two children up on the castle walls – just this morning. And what did I hear? I heard them talk about MERRION'S MEAD! I could hardly believe my ears. One of them actually stood up and *bellowed* at me that he could make monsters with magic Merrion's Mead! Yes!"

Aunt Thea groaned. It had to be Lewis. He was always loudly talking about their Tauronian adventures, knowing that nobody would ever believe they were true. Who would have guessed that one day he'd do it within earshot of the one man in the country who *would* believe?

"So, I followed them down through the castle, listening in, and found out all about the wonderful Aunt Thea who allowed them to keep the mead – *my* mead – safe in her kitchen cupboard. And then I saw their lovely parents write their details in a Friends of Trindle Castle application form. And, lo and behold, they fill in the Recommend a Friend & Get 10% Off box. And the friend they recommend is one

Aramathea Casterbridge! Aunt Thea herself! Name and address, neatly supplied. It was a sign. A sign, I tell you! The mead was meant for me! I was always destined for greatness. Always!" He stared intensely up into a dark corner of the stone room, one hand outstretched, the other at his heart.

"Oo-K," said Aunt Thea. Clearly the man was having a bit of a personal moment.

He suddenly broke off from his staring. "Okeydoke," he said. "Give it to her, boys."

The henchmen – one with curly black hair and a small gold earring and the other with a ginger beard – advanced upon her menacingly.

And gave her a writing pad and a ballpoint pen.

"What's this for?" she spluttered. "Do you want me to write a diary entry? It won't be lady-like."

"No," said Lord Merrion, with a smug smile. "I want you to invite little Jack and Lewis over to play. At your place. Tomorrow morning. My boys will deliver the note to their home and when they skip along to your cottage tomorrow, we will collect them."

"But why? What do you want with them?" said Aunt Thea. "You've got the mead. Just let me go and you'll never hear from any of us again. I'll be glad to be rid of it, to be honest," she added. "It's nothing but trouble."

"Ah, but it's not that simple, is it?" he said. "I don't know if this is *all* of it. And I demand to have *all* of it! Now, I *could* search your home, but I would never be sure that I had it all. But if I've got your nephews, I know you'll tell me the truth!"

"I already have. You've got it all," said Aunt Thea, with a squeaky edge to her voice.

"Well then, tomorrow we'll find out! Write the note please."

"But I would normally just phone their parents," she said. "They would think a note was very odd."

"Ah, but we ripped out your phone line, just before we all left," grinned Lord Merrion, looking very impressed with himself. "So you can explain that it's out of order and you just dropped a note in while you were passing. We know they've gone out for the evening, you see.

This is a *plan*, you know!"

Aunt Thea looked down at the blank page, picked up the pen, took a deep breath and began to write.

# Chapter 4

# Men Tek Zem All

Jack and Lewis stared up at Ninjataur in amazement and then with growing horror as they realized what he had just said.

"She and leetle boddles ... men tek zem all. . ."

If Lewis hadn't given him a very bad mixed up accent of "Japanese warrior" and "Russian spy" when he'd meaded him, Ninjataur would probably have said: "She and little bottles – men take them all."

"What men? Who? Where did they take her?" they both gabbled, as Ninjataur swung down from the light fitting and dropped silently to the floor.

"Men tek her. In white van. Theess all I know. I hide. Hide on the silling."

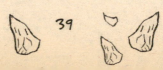

"But what are you *doing* here?" burst out Lewis, astonished to find his Taur still not back in Tauronia after the very thorough meading he'd got only half an hour ago.

"I kem home," Ninjataur grinned. They could tell by the way his cheeks bunched up under the silk mask, and his eyes swivelled from side to side.

"Not *this* home! *Your* home!" said Lewis. Ninjataur shrugged. Lewis remembered he had been thinking of getting back to Aunt Thea's warm kitchen and having a hot drink, even while he was sighing with relief and pouring the mead back in the wood. He was really going to have to concentrate harder in future. Merrion's Mead magic could be very slippery at times.

"Just as well, though," said Jack. "We need help – and right now Ninjataur is the only help we've got. We can't mead up Electrotaur or Slashermite – or any other Taur or Mite at all. There's no mead left." He gulped. "Whoever these men were, they came for the mead. And they took Aunt Thea too."

"What shall we do?" Lewis stared up at his

brother, his blue eyes big with worry.

Jack stared at the floor for a few seconds, trying to work out a plan – and then he shook his head, walked across to the phone and picked up the receiver. "We have to call the police," he said.

Lewis stared at him gravely. Through all the adventures of the past few months – lost monsters, electrical catastrophes, mind-control, escaped floral killing machines . . . they had *never* once called the police. The police were from the real world. They would never understand or believe the world of Tauronia or Merrion's Mead – and the amazing things that came out of it.

But this was different. Aunt Thea hadn't been attacked by sulky Dragomites or chased by deadly finger-knitting. She had been kidnapped by normal humans.

Jack put the receiver to his ear, and then clicked the buttons on the cradle several times. He frowned. "It's . . . it's not working," he said. "It's disconnected."

"We need another phone," said Lewis. "One of the neighbours?"

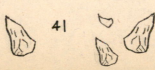

"No. They'll think we're just messing around," said Jack. "We'll have to run back home."

"But what about *him?*" Lewis pointed at Ninjataur who was now crouched on top of the sofa, gradually changing to the same green and red tartan pattern as its cushions.

Jack sighed. If only the last Taur left in the Overworld had been a bit more useful. If they had managed to keep Dragotaur they could be up soaring over the clouds by now, trying to spot a white van driving along the roads nearby.

"We'll have to take him with us," he said. "We'll go through the woods where nobody will see him. He can camouflage himself, anyway, if anyone comes along. But you make sure you don't lose him again, Lew! This is serious. We might need him. Come on, we haven't got any time to waste!"

Lewis took Ninjataur's silk-clad hand and gripped it hard. "Listen to me, Ninjataur. I am your creator. You must do exactly what I say — do you understand?" His Taur nodded. "Good. Then come with us and *never* run off on your own again!"

They checked left and right outside the house

before darting across the road, splashing through the shallow river and running into the wood.

"What if we never find her?" puffed Lewis, hopping over a fallen log.

"We will!" huffed Jack. "We have to."

"And what if we've lost the mead for ever? We'll never see Electrotaur and Slashermite again. . ." Lewis gulped.

"Or any of the others," panted Jack. "What about Tryangletaur? I only made him last week and I never even got a chance to get him up to help with my Maths homework!"

Jack had made Tryangletaur when he should have been doing his homework on angles. He'd thought having a Taur with special angle-working-out powers might help, but Mum had phoned to ask them to go home before Aunt Thea could let him bring Tryangletaur up from Tauronia with Slashermite. Aunt Thea wouldn't let them meet *every* new Taur or Mite they made, but every so often, if they promised that the monster wasn't dangerous, she'd agree. Slashermite would accompany the new creature up and make sure it knew how to behave.

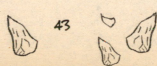

"At least we've still got Ninjataur!" said Lewis, leaping over a clump of brambles. "And that's brilliant!"

"Is he still there?" asked Jack, squinting around them.

"Yes," said Lewis. "He's right behind us." Ninjataur was at Lewis's heels, silent and agile. "I've told him to stay close to us at all times. I'm his master. He'll do what I say."

"But is he OK? I mean, did you draw him to suddenly dissolve or catch fire or anything? Can you remember all his powers and weaknesses and stuff?"

Lewis frowned, thinking. It was some time ago that he had drawn Ninjataur. "Umm. . . No – I'm sure he's just a ninja."

"No weaknesses or funny habits?" Jack knew Lewis sometimes thought up some pretty bizarre stuff for his Taurs or Mites. Raptotaur, for example, might be a vicious killer, but he liked to wear jam sandwiches on his ears and would melt if human dribble touched him.

"No, he's just a ninja," said Lewis. "A silent, incredibly fast fighting machine. And an expert

in camouflage. That's all."

They reached the edge of the wood and followed the alley that led into their road alongside their back garden fence. Lewis made Ninjataur hop over it and wait on the lawn. Once they'd got into the house, using the spare key that their mum hid in the garden, they let him in through the back door.

For a second they all stood still in the neat, modern kitchen, staring at each other. Then Jack said, "Phone!" and made for the hallway. Halfway along it he froze.

Someone was lurking outside the front door and pushing something through the letterbox. A handwritten note fluttered to the carpet and Jack snatched it up immediately. Lewis ran to read it with him.

The note was written in blue biro, with lots of curls and little hearts over the "i"s. It read:

Darling Jack and Lewis

Please come over to play in the

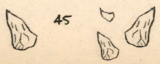

45

*morning at ten a.m. Tell Mum I can't phone — the number's out of order. Do come! If you do we can have Battenberg cake, Lewis — your favourite! And liquorice for you, Jack! See you then...*

*Love and cuddles, Aunty Thea*

Lewis and Jack gaped at each other. "I *hate* Battenberg – she knows that!" breathed Lewis.

"And *I* hate liquorice!" said Jack.

"And what about all those curls and hearts? And '*love and cuddles*'?" grimaced Lewis.

"It's a warning!" said Jack. "She was made to write it!" He tore open the front door and ran down the path to the kerb. Turning the corner at the far end of the road was a white van. "Lew! It's them! The kidnappers! We've got to follow them!"

Jack was about to run after the van but Lewis grabbed his arm. "No, Jack! This way! Ninji – follow us!" Ninjataur slid out of the

front door, shimmering with camouflage. It fell shut behind him as he shot after Jack and Lewis who were running up the side passage and back into the cutway.

*Of course!* thought Jack. *We can cut through a corner of the wood and join the road further along, in time to see the white van.*

A minute later they ran out of the trees and reached the road. "Oh no!" wailed Jack. He could see no sign of a van of any colour driving along the quiet street.

"Yes!" hissed Lewis, beside him, pointing to the corner shop, across the road. A white van was parked by it – and getting out of it were two shifty-looking men in boiler suits.

Jack and Lewis scuttled across the road, crouching low in case the men looked back as they headed into the shop. Ninjataur cleared the road in one leap. One second he was a flickering shape made of grass, the next he had camouflaged himself to match the slightly grubby white of the van.

Jack peered in through the windows. "Is this it, Ninji?" he whispered.

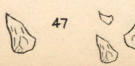

"Yez – ees eet," murmured Ninjataur, right in his ear. Jack jumped, realizing that the creature was flat against the sliding van door.

"And did you recognize the men?" asked Lewis, in an urgent whisper, eyeing the door of the corner shop across the wing mirror.

"Yez – ees ze men," confirmed his creation.

"I can't see anyone inside here," said Jack, putting on his spectacles and straining to see past the seats to the back. There were two more seats behind the driver and passenger seats, but the back of the van seemed to be mostly empty.

He could only see an old grey blanket, a spare tyre and a bit of frayed rope.

"We have to get in," he said. "Stow away."

"But they'll see us!" said Lew.

"We'll keep down low," said Jack. "It's our only hope of finding out where they took Aunt Thea!"

Lewis nodded and tried the driver's door. It was locked. "Now what?" he said. Jack edged around and tried the back door. That was locked too. He groaned with frustration.

Then there was a movement beside him and a flash of silver. Ninjataur, still camouflaged as the van's grubby white paintwork, its yellow number plate seeming to glide across his knees like a projected film, was picking the lock with the sharp point of his ninjato. Three seconds later the door fell open – just as the tinkling bell of the corner shop door announced that the men were coming back.

Jack and Lewis jumped inside the van and Ninjataur followed, sliding his short sword back into his belt. Jack pulled the back door shut, swiftly and quietly, behind them, and they all

dropped to the dusty metal floor of the van. Lewis's heart rattled hard in his chest as the front doors were pulled open and the men got in. If they glanced back just once they would see their stowaways. Then Lewis felt a coolness on his head and back and realized that Ninjataur had put his silken arms across the boys on either side of him. He grinned with delight, suddenly remembering. Of course! Ninjataur could also make other things go into camouflage by touching them!

With a strange tickly feeling, Jack turned into a tyre and Lewis became a folded blanket.

# Chapter 5

# Welsh Warbling Torture

Aunt Thea was disappointed. Obviously she was worried, in fear for her life, stressed about the plan to capture Jack and Lewis – all of these things – but, most of all she felt disappointed.

Lord Merrion should never have looked like *this*. Lord Merrion was such an upright, noble, commanding kind of name. He should be tall with broad angular shoulders. His eyes should be steely and determined. His jaw should be firm. Even if he was evil, he might at least have been all these things. But no. Just her luck. Lord Merrion was a dumpy, podgy, greasy little man, not much taller than she was, with thin, oily hair and a tendency to flush and perspire. He made no attempt at all to be tall, angular and good-looking and it was really beginning to annoy her.

"Are you *really* Lord Merrion?" she asked as he paced up and down the dungeon in front of her, humming tunelessly and clutching one of the bottles of mead while he plotted his evil deeds. For turning a perfectly lovely castle into a tacky theme park was pretty evil in Aunt Thea's book. Nearly as bad as kidnapping.

His pink sweaty face snapped around to stare at her angrily. "Of course I am he! Who says I'm not?!"

"Hmm – touchy," observed Aunt Thea.

"I am he! Did anyone say I wasn't?" Lord Merrion persisted, looking petulant.

"Of course not. Why? Might they?"

"I *am* the great great great gr—"

"Yes, yes, I've heard how great you are. Have to say I think your greatness is somewhat overrated. A *true* gentleman would not tie a lady's hands behind her back. Why don't you just mead me into being nice and calm, instead?"

"*Mead* you?" Lord Merrion paused and

then uncorked the little bottle before looking furtively into it.

"Well, yes! It is magic after all. And if you could just magic mead me into a more comfortable position and more cheerful mood, I would be ever so grateful."

He tilted his head to one side and stared at her, like a confused starling.

"Don't you *know* how to mead?" she asked, suppressing a grin. Until now, it had not occurred to her that he might not know what to do with it.

"I *drink* the mead," he said. "And then I dream of my wonderful castle theme park. And then it all comes true! All of it! And I don't have to spend a penny more on any workmen! And people will flock from all over the world and pay to come in and I will be rich, rich, RICH!"

"O . . . K," said Aunt Thea. "Well . . . go right ahead. What's stopping you?"

The lord hesitated, peering at the bottle, and then placed it back in the box. "I am *waiting* for the *right moment*! And that's not

until I am certain that I have all the mead you stole from me back again. Once your nephews are here I can threaten each of you in turn to make sure the others tell me *everything*! Then I will know for sure that I have all the mead back in my family. And then – and only *then* – I will make my dreams come true!" He burst triumphantly into more tuneless humming.

Aunt Thea winced. "Do you *have* to do that?" she asked.

He stopped again and looked haughty. "I, madam, am the most esteemed singer in the

Merrion Welsh Male Voice Choir! You are *privileged* to hear me perform! I am on CDs, I am! In fact, here," he fumbled through his pockets and produced a shiny silver disc in a plastic sleeve, "here is my own composition! The choir will sing this at harvest festival! And I have recorded it — all with my own voice on lots of tracks. Listen!"

He suddenly turned and went to a tall dresser type thing which had a portable CD player on it, next to the box of mead bottles. He flung the CD into the machine and in no time at all the stone dungeon was reverberating to the intense melody of a Welsh Male Voice Choir. This would normally be a lovely thing. But in *this* case it was not. The "choir" was made up entirely of Lord Merrion's reedy off tune voice, recorded over and over and then squashed together in an offence against the human ear. It was ghastly. Aunt Thea's left eye began to twitch. Paint began to peel off the dungeon door.

"You see!" he crowed. "You see! I *am* the Merrion Welsh Male Voice Choir!" And he

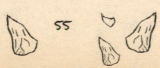

joined in lustily with his CD before looking at his watch, putting the mead bottle back in the box with the others, and marching off out of the room yodelling like a cracked recorder. He left the CD playing.

"Oh great," muttered Aunt Thea, trying to work her hands loose. "Torture."

## Chapter 6

# Van Drive Through Hell

"Wagon Wheels," said the one with the ginger beard, sitting in the passenger seat, "are definitely smaller than they used to be."

The one with curly black hair and an earring grunted.

"I tell you, they used to be like dinner plates," went on the ginger-bearded one. "You couldn't jam 'em all in your gob in one go, but now – look!" He jammed the large, round biscuit into his mouth and spoke through it: "Sh'easy! You can put 'em in whole! Vey are definitely shmaller!"

"As it ever occurred to you, Clint?" said the driver, "that your gob's just got bigger?"

"That is rude, Wayne," said Clint, shovelling another chocolate mallow treat in.

Jack and Lewis tried not to giggle. They were camouflaged but they might still be heard.

"Anyway, I need the sugar!" muttered Clint. "After doin' all this dirty work for his lordship. That red-haired witch nearly kicked my kneecaps off on the way to the castle."

Jack and Lewis both gasped. The castle? Lewis peered between the two back seats and recognized the ginger-bearded one – Clint – now. "It's one of the workmen who was up on the battlements of Trindle Castle this morning!" he whispered to Jack.

"She thumped *me* on the nose," Wayne was saying. "She's a nutter! Mind you, so is he. What's all that about, eh? Magic mead? Some kid starts talking about making monsters and we all have to go off burgling and kidnapping. He's a nutter, too. No mistake."

"What's he gonna do with her and those brats when he gets 'em, anyway?" said Clint. "Drop 'em in the moat? Lock 'em in the top tower 'til they go mouldy?"

"I don't care what he does with 'em. Let's just get our money and get off this job," said

Wayne. "Sharpish. We can go straight out and pick the kids up in the morning, hand 'em over and then make him give us double pay to make sure we don't tell nobody nuffin. Then we're out of it! Now . . . let's go home. I've had enough of castles and nutters for one day."

Jack grabbed Lewis's shoulder. "We've got to make them take us to the castle – now!" he hissed. "We can't wait in this van all night!"

Lewis nodded and had a word with Ninjataur.

"So, you got any of those Wagon Wheels left?" asked Wayne. He hadn't noticed the movement in the back seats as Jack and Lewis climbed into them and put on seat belts. Ninjataur crouched between them and slid his hand down to his side.

Clint, though, felt suddenly uneasy. He could have sworn he just saw a pair of silver eyes floating in the air to his right.

"Oy – hand one over, you gutbucket!" said Wayne, pausing at some traffic lights.

"Eeeeeeeem," said Clint, as Jack, Lewis and Ninjataur all suddenly de-camouflaged in the

seats behind them.

"Stay calm," said Lewis. "And my monster won't kill you. Probably."

The screaming went on for quite a while, but eventually Wayne pulled away from the traffic lights, whimpering.

"Roo-oo-gleeeeyupp!" said Clint, his eyes bulging in panic as Wayne drove over a traffic calming bump. Ninjataur's blade had been jogged nastily against his throat.

"All right, Ninji," said Lewis. "You can hold the blade a couple of inches away from his neck. You don't want to cut his throat by accident, do you? Only when I actually *tell* you to."

"What *is* that thing?" squeaked Wayne, gripping the steering wheel so hard his knuckles were turning white. Little beads of sweat stood out on his forehead and every so often he would let go of the steering wheel with one hand and pinch his left earlobe, while muttering.

"It's a Taur," said Lewis. "From Tauronia. I made him. You probably know how."

The workmen glanced at each other. All they really knew was that their boss was slightly

mad, not above a bit of kidnap, and seemed to think a bit of old brewed honey had magical properties. They were beginning to wish they'd stuck to repointing the stonework.

"So, the man who's kidnapped our aunt. Who is he – and what does he want?" demanded Jack, trying his best to sound calm and in control when his heart was racing and he had to keep gulping with the excitement and worry of it all.

"Look, son, we don't know anything," said Wayne. "We were just meant to bring you to the castle tomorrow. We'd have picked you up today, but you went off out in the car with your folks. We wouldn't have 'urt you or nuffin, though. We wouldn't 'urt a fly, would we, Clint?"

"Eeeyyerrweeeble," said Clint.

"What castle?" asked Jack.

"Trindle Castle," gulped Wayne, his eyes sliding fearfully around towards Ninjataur. "You were both there this morning. You were talking about some mead stuff and the boss heard you. He said it was his and you'd stolen it. All right?"

"So why didn't he come after us?" asked Lewis, beginning to feel rather guilty. Aunt Thea getting kidnapped, he now realized, was *his* fault.

"He did. He followed you back to your mum and dad earlier, and then found out who you were and where you lived when they filled in the Friends of Trindle Castle form. They put your aunt's details in the Recommend a Friend bit too . . . and he'd heard you say you kept the mead at your auntie's place. So we went round her's—"

"And you just broke in and stole it and then kidnapped her!" Jack snapped. He felt furious. Ninjataur glanced across at Jack and then Lewis. From behind his silk mask he hissed, "You wan I keel hem?" and waved his blade in the direction of Wayne. Wayne shrieked and began working his earlobe again, muttering frantically. The van swerved a little in the road.

"Nah," said Lewis. "Not until I say so, OK, Ninjataur?" Ninjataur managed to look disappointed even with his mask on. His eyes

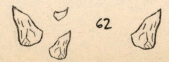

narrowed and a little bloom of silk blew out as he released a short sigh.

"Look, we was just doing what we was told," bleated Clint. "And she came quietly – eventually."

"You still haven't told us who your boss is," said Lewis. "Is he the owner of Trindle Castle?"

"Yeah," said Wayne. "Calls himself Lord Merrion."

Jack and Lewis both sat up in shock and gasped, "What?!" Ninjataur immediately flicked his sword across to Wayne's throat and the driver shrieked again and took his hands off the wheel.

"No! Ninjataur!" shouted Lewis, while Jack leaped forward and grabbed the wheel. He wrestled with it and got the van back straight on the road just before it veered into a ditch.

"*Notrealit'snotrealit'snotreal. . .*" Wayne was gibbering, his eyes shut, rubbing his left earlobe again.

"Open your eyes! Take the wheel!" yelled Jack. Thankfully, Wayne did as he was told.

As he steadied the van and drove on along what was, thankfully, a deserted country lane, Jack shook his head. "What is it with you and your earlobe?" he asked.

"It's how I handle stress," mumbled Wayne.

## Chapter 7

# Bang Goes That Idea

"I must stress," said Lord Merrion, "that *I* am not the baddie here!"

"Right," said Aunt Thea. "So getting kidnapped and tied up is all my own fault, then."

"You stole my birthright!" he insisted.

"Bought it," corrected Aunt Thea. "Think I even have a receipt somewhere. And if your family is so careless with it that it ends up in a gift shop next to the decorative leek badges and the funny black hats, well that's your bad luck. Should have looked after it better."

"No matter!" He smiled smugly and turned away, walking towards the dresser. Aunt Thea felt a stab of alarm. Was he going to put the Merrion's Male Voice Choir CD on again? She

wasn't sure she could stand another rendition of "Glorious Lord Of The Valleys" (Merrion's own composition). She had always enjoyed Welsh male voice choirs until now. She might be put off for life after today.

But no. He was just lovingly opening the box which contained all the little bottles of mead. "Soon – soon!" he crooned. "I will have the power!" He did a little dance and punched the air.

Then he fished out his mobile phone and stepped across to the doorway where a shaft of daylight fell into the stairwell from the castle courtyard above. They were in a section of the castle shut off to visitors – but as it was after five p.m., the tourist part of the building was now shut in any case.

"Well, have you delivered the note?" she heard Merrion shout. "What? Good! Speak up man. You sound like you're being strangled! What? Look – just get back here. I need you to stand guard over this blasted aunt tonight – and then fetch those boys in the morning. Don't worry, you'll get paid overtime. Tomorrow I will

meet *my destiny!*" The phone was snapped shut and Lord Merrion began to sing again. A little more paint peeled off the door and a family of mice abruptly left their nest under the dresser, deciding to take their chances with the courtyard cat.

"Good. Well done," said Jack, putting Wayne's mobile phone in his pocket. They had listened to Lord Merrion on speaker phone and Wayne had answered him as normally as possible, given that Ninjataur had been holding him firmly by the throat, while his spare hand kept the ninjato blade a few centimetres from Clint's neck.

Lewis was grinning from ear to ear. He was having a *great* time. They were going to rescue Aunt Thea and nothing could stop them. His Taur was amazing and could not be defeated! Thank goodness he had drawn Ninjataur so brilliantly and given him such useful talents.

Only one thing niggled at Lewis. After Jack's question in the woods, he had been trying to remember what Ninjataur's weakness was. Most Taurs and Mites had some kind

of weakness. They were usually rather odd weaknesses – and you really had to know what they were because you would never guess them. For example, Tundrataur could be defeated by dairy. Tundrataur was the marathon runner of Tauronia and would yomp endlessly across the Tauronian Tundra, eating insects as he went and grabbing handfuls of snow to keep himself hydrated. Almost nothing could stop him. Except cheese. Just the *smell* of cheese would bring him to his knees. Now Lavataur, while he couldn't be stopped by water (he was far too hot for that and it just turned into steam before it ever got near him) *could* be cooled down and temporarily immobilized by the ice breath of a female Frostomite. Assuming you could persuade a female Frostomite to help out. They were notoriously sulky and unhelpful. . .

Electrotaur could be turned off if you hit the button on the middle of his chest. It was more of a safety feature than anything else, but it had saved lives before now. The thing was, you had to *know* all of this, which of course, Jack and Lewis *did*.

Except when they had forgotten. And when it came to Ninjataur, drawn and meaded to life so long ago, Lewis *had* . . . kind of . . . forgotten. Still. No need to worry. Ninjataur was going to help them rescue Aunt Thea and get the mead back and then they would put everything right and go home for supper.

"We're here now," croaked Wayne, pulling off the road on to a track that led away from the main castle gate and its ticket office and turnstile, around a back lane, to the staff and deliveries entrance. The sky was darkening now, in the early autumn evening, and the moat gleamed navy blue as they drove past. Nobody was about as they approached a small wooden bridge that led over the water and through a modest stone archway in the thick grey stone wall of the outer keep.

The van rolled through the archway and across the cobbles of the old courtyard, turning left and parking close to the wall. "Right," said Jack, trying hard to sound as if he knew what he was doing. "I want you to take us to Lord Merrion, as if you've just found us here and

captured us – all right? Ninjataur will follow us, but he'll be camouflaged and nobody will see him. At first."

The men nodded anxiously. Wayne rubbed his earlobe frantically.

"Ninjataur will not hurt you unless I tell him to," said Lewis. "I only have to give him a signal, so don't try anything or he'll snap your heads off."

The men nodded again. "I've had enough of this job," squeaked Clint, with one hand clutched nervously to his throat. "Why don't you just let us go? We'll get right out of here and won't come back. And we won't tell no one."

"Nope. Not yet," said Jack. He knew that, whatever happened, these men would have to be hypnotized by Slashermite to forget about Ninjataur. Nobody could know the secret of Merrion's Mead. It was just too dangerous.

They all jumped out of the van and for a moment Clint and Wayne stood about uneasily, not sure what to do. Ninjataur stepped behind them and then vanished from view as he

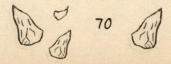

camouflaged himself to look like the rock walls of the courtyard. If you looked carefully, you could still see his outline glinting when he moved.

"Right, come on!" urged Jack. "Make it good." The men looked at each other, glanced fearfully over their shoulders, and then took Jack and Lewis by their arms and began to propel them towards a green painted door which stood open in the far wall of the courtyard. A light shone up from it.

Soon they were going down the stone steps to the floor below. "Boss, you'll never believe it," called out Wayne, in a voice that trembled. Jack hoped Lord Merrion wouldn't notice. "We've just found them kids sneaking around outside!"

"Get off! Get off me!" shouted Jack, with a wink at Clint, who looked miserable and pale behind his beard.

"Unhand me, you villain!" added Lewis, smothering a giggle. Jack shot him a *look*. They mustn't give the game away yet.

At the foot of the steps, Clint and Wayne

71

steered them into an open doorway to their left and down a few more steps into a dungeon-like room. Aunt Thea was there, sitting up straight on a wooden chair with her hands behind her back. She lifted her chin and smiled at them.

Beside her stood a rather podgy, sweaty-looking man in an ill-fitting suit. "So!" he cried, looking first incredulous and then smugly thrilled. "You saved us the trouble of capturing you tomorrow. And now my destiny hurtles towards me ever faster!"

Aunt Thea winced. "The dialogue doesn't get any better," she warned her nephews.

"At last, the time has come for me to reclaim my birthright!" added Lord Merrion, sweeping his arm up into the air and then, after a moment, realizing it had nothing much to do up there, letting it drop back down again.

"What *are* you on about?" said Lewis. "Why have you kidnapped Aunt Thea?"

"As if you didn't know!" said Lord Merrion. "Why, you *told* me yourself, this morning – didn't you? You yelled it from the ramparts – that *you've* got the Merrion's Mead! That

72

*she* brought it to you! That you are *using* its magic!"

Lewis sighed and shoved his hands into his pockets. "You've got a point," he admitted. "So now what?"

"So now!" Merrion stepped towards them, glowering. "I claim back what is MINE! I—" A sudden high-pitched ring cut through his proclamation and he dug out his mobile phone with an irritated huff. He flipped it open. "Yeah? What?" he said. And then his lower lip stuck out. "Oh, it's *you*! *No*. No, I'm *not* in. Look, I'm in the middle of something right now. No. I don't *want* you to visit. . . Because this is *my* castle! Mine! And you're not allowed in. So don't you come! Go back to your *own* castle!" He snapped the phone shut with a mew of annoyance and then shoved it back in his pocket. "So . . . where was I? Ah yes – I claim back what is MINE!"

Jack looked around. "So, you've nicked the mead then."

"I haven't *nicked* anything! It belongs to me. All of it! And now that I have you all here, I

will find out where the rest of it is!"

"I've already told you," sighed Aunt Thea. "You've got it all. There isn't any more."

"And why should I believe you?" said Lord Merrion. "That's why you're all here. If you won't tell me the truth. . ." he grabbed Lewis's arm and pulled him in front of Aunt Thea. . . "it will go very badly for this one!" Aunt Thea clamped her mouth shut and her nostrils flared. Jack could see she was furious and scared for Lewis. But Lewis laughed. Lord Merrion couldn't see Wayne and Clint's terrified expressions and kicking legs as Ninjataur picked them both up by their collars and hung them both on some high coat pegs which were nailed into the dungeon wall.

"Come on, Ninji!" he giggled. "I think it's time you did your thing. No killing, though – OK?"

Lord Merrion frowned in confusion and peered down at Lewis. Then Ninjataur bloomed back into view, inches from his face. His silver eyes were glittering with delight as he grabbed hold of the loathsome lord and began to spin him in the air.

"AAAAAAAAAAAAARRRRRRRGH!" screamed Lord Merrion, his face awash with terror and his mouth sending out a small shower of spit as he spun past – rather like a garden sprinkler.

"Yey!" cried Lewis. "Spin him, Ninji! Spin the Baddie!"

Ninjataur spun the lord around and around, like a clunky, sweaty lasso. The Taur's slender silk-clad arms were incredibly strong and it was no effort for him at all.

The lord continued to scream and shriek while his arms and legs flailed out in all directions. Up on the coat hooks Wayne and Clint were wailing with fright. Wayne's collar was tearing and he was now sliding down the wall, but he was too scared to try to run away.

Aunt Thea was hooting with laughter. "Ninjataur! How on earth? Oh! You clever boys!"

*It was glorious*, thought Jack. He could even see all the little bottles of mead in an open box next to a CD player on top of a dresser. Soon the lord would be a semi-conscious ga-ga heap on the ground and they'd be able to collect their mead and take it safely home. They could make the workmen drive them all back and then get Slashermite up to hypnotize the lot of them to forget the whole thing – and all before supper. They'd done it!

He ducked as Lord Merrion's left foot flew past his ear on its high speed arc and then there was a thud as it made contact with the stuff on the dresser. Jack's heart lurched as the box full of bottles of mead tumbled sideways. He

threw himself across the room and saved it just in the nick of time. But as he did so his elbow connected with the buttons on top of the CD player and all of a sudden the room was flooded with some truly dreadful noise. The Merrion Male Voice Choir CD was still in the machine and now booming horribly out of the speakers.

For a few seconds they all stood, stunned. It was all they could hear. Some truly dreadful, out of tune, out of time, fog-horny wailing so bad that no amount of charming Welsh lilt could improve it.

Ninjataur seemed to be frozen, holding the dizzy Lord Merrion up in both hands and going slightly cross-eyed.

Then there was a very loud bang.

Lord Merrion was suddenly lying dazed on the floor.

Ninjataur had exploded.

## Chapter 8

# Getting the Point

"Ah," said Lewis. "That would be the bad singing. I remember now. Bad singing is Ninjataur's weakness. Sing *really* out of tune at him and he . . . kind of . . . pops."

"Pops?!" spluttered Jack, peeling bits of Ninjataur off his jumper. "You made a Taur that *pops*?! Well done, Lew! Oh well done!"

"Erm," said Aunt Thea, but they didn't take any notice.

"Well how was I to know that we were stumbling into a bad singing trap?" squawked Lewis, picking bits of Ninjataur out of his hair. "How was I to know that *the worst singing in the world* was just waiting here in this dungeon? And *you* switched it on! YOU made him pop!"

"Um," added Aunt Thea, but they paid her no heed.

"This is the *last* time I take you on a rescue!" snapped Jack, flicking bits of Ninjataur off his trousers. "Your Taurs just can't be trusted! I mean, how on earth did you come up with a stupid idea like *that*? Suppose one of *us* had started singing?! He was just a ninja time bomb ready to go off at any moment!"

"But we sing in *tune*!" protested Lewis, unravelling a rather stringy bit of Ninjataur from his shoe.

"*I* SING IN TUNE!" boomed an outraged voice just behind them. "HEAR ME SING WITH TRIUMPH! FOR NOW I *WILL* CLAIM MY BIRTHRIGHT!"

"Ah," said Lewis. Seconds later he was seized by his arms and hauled backwards. He was flung on to a chair next to Aunt Thea and his hands were tied tightly behind his back. Next to him, Jack was getting the same treatment. Clint and Wayne had got off their hooks and were gleefully helping Lord Merrion to truss up their prisoners. Clint put his ginger face close to

79

Lewis and sneered, "Don't worry about Wayne, he won't hurt you, unless I tell him to!"

"Now," gasped Lord Merrion, standing back to look at the three of them. He was covered in Ninjataur goo and tiny frayed scraps of blue silk. He'd taken the brunt of the blast. "Let's get this over and done with. I want to know where the rest of the mead is. And you are going to tell me."

"I've already told you," said Aunt Thea, shaking her head wearily. "You've got it all. We used up the first two bottles very fast because they got knocked over. Then I rang up the shopkeeper and got him to send me the rest. Six of them arrived by taxi and since then we've used up nearly another three. The three full ones and one with just a tiny bit in it are all that's left."

"So, you're trying to tell me that you knew this was magic – and all the things it could do – and it never occurred to you to *hide* any of it?" sneered Lord Merrion.

Aunt Thea looked shamefaced. "No. It never did. Because nobody else on this planet would ever *believe* it was magic."

"Apart from a couple of girls at school,"

mentioned Lewis.

"And a BBC reporter," added Jack.

"And a cameraman," listed Lewis.

"But we hypnotized all of them," said Jack. "They don't know anything about it. Nobody knows."

"Except me! I know it *all*!" murmured Lord Merrion, inflating his chest in an important way. "Heir to the Merrion destiny!" He certainly looked as if he believed them, and Aunt Thea sighed with relief. Perhaps he wouldn't hurt Jack and Lewis after all.

"So," pondered the heir to the Merrion destiny. "You are *quite* certain there is no more hidden away. Do not lie to me, because I can tell, you know . . . I can tell!"

"None at all," said Aunt Thea, looking him squarely in the eye. "You have it all in that box over there. . ." The lord looked smug.

"Except. . ." said Lewis. The lord's eyes flicked across to him, narrowing suspiciously. "I think—"

"Lewis! There is no more!" said Aunt Thea, alarmed.

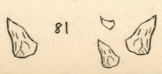

"Well, there kind of is," said Lew, ignoring Jack's urgent face pulling to get him to shut up.

"Where?" demanded the lord.

"Well, it's all over our pictures," said Lewis. "And, I mean, it is dried up and probably no good now, but ... well, Merrion's Mead is soaked into the paper. If we made the paper wet again, it might still be magic."

Aunt Thea and Jack stared at him, aghast, wondering what he was doing.

"Where are these drawings?" asked Lord Merrion.

"Back at Aunt Thea's," said Lewis. "All over the house really – in lots of different places. Even some out in the garden. We just draw them and spill mead on them and drop them. That's how we bring our monsters to life. I think I can remember where all the pictures are, though. Let's go back and we'll find them for you."

"It sounds like a trap, boss," said Wayne, rubbing his earlobe while he scuffed a rather blubbery bit of Ninjataur off his trainer.

"Yes, I rather think it does. What if your aunt's house is hiding some other creatures like the

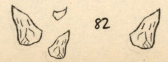

82

unlucky one that's dripping off my ceiling now?"

"Oh no," said Jack. "We're not allowed to have any Taurs or Mites in the house. They all live in an underground world called Tauronia and they can't get out unless we mead them out – and only if Aunt Thea says so."

"It's true," nodded Aunt Thea. "Taurs play havoc with my soft furnishings."

"Take him," said Lord Merrion, pointing to Lewis. "Clint, drive him back to the house and get all the pictures. And this time, don't let him get the better of you! He's just one snotty little six-year-old squirt. You ought to be able to manage!"

"Oy! I'm nearly eight!" protested Lewis as Clint undid his tied hands.

"Now remember, boyo," warned the lord. "If you don't get back here by. . ." he looked at his watch. . . "seven-thirty, I'll have a go at this drawing lark myself. Thanks for tipping me off! Drawing all my plans is a *much* better way of making my dreams come to life. But if you don't come back on time I'll start with a drawing of your brother and your aunt turning into worms.

 83

I'll magic mead it, watch them turn into little writhing pink beasties – and then stamp on them!"

Lewis nodded soberly, but as Clint grabbed him by the arm and yanked him up the steps he glanced back at Jack and Aunt Thea and gave them a secret wink and a grin. He was up to something. Definitely.

Lord Merrion and Wayne followed Clint up and out to the van, to make sure Lewis was securely put into it. Jack and Aunt Thea were left alone. "I'm so sorry, Jack," she said. "I am *such* a bad aunt. I should never, ever, have allowed all this mead madness to go on. We should have learned our lesson last time when Flowertaur escaped and started firing deadly poison thorns at your enemies."

"It all worked out OK. Nobody died in the end."

"Yes . . . but even so. I really think whatever happens now, our Merrion's Mead adventures must come to an end."

Lord Merrion strode back down the stone steps. "So!" he said. "You've got ninety minutes! Ninety minutes before I magic mead you into worms and grind you under the heel of my boot! Or maybe not, if your nephew comes back with all the pictures as he promised. Maybe then I will just magic mead you all into my servants. Yes, I rather like that idea. I don't *drink* the mead – I draw what I want and spill mead drops on to it. Yes, that sounds much better . . . it'll last longer." He peered at them both with a smug grin. "You'd make a great floor scrubber and bin emptier," he said to Jack. "And your brother could clean my chimneys by crawling up them – and you – *dear* lady, could be my cook! Working eighteen hours a days, seven days a week . . . for ever! Aha! A ha ha ha ha ha!" He ran back up the stairs – flinging back his arm as if he was throwing a long black cloak over his shoulder. He didn't actually have one, but it was very obvious that he was imagining he had.

Silence reigned in the dungeon, broken only by the occasional plopping of Ninjataur goo as it fell off the ceiling on to the stone floor. It smelled of pear drops.

"Jack," said Aunt Thea, after a few seconds. "How bendy are you?"

"Um . . . what?"

"Are you any good at gymnastics?"

"Not bad. Why?" Jack wondered if Aunt Thea was going a bit barmy with the strain. He wouldn't blame her.

"Well, you see, if *I* shuffle forward like *this*. . ." she jumped up and down in her seat, as far as she was able and clattered her chair forward a few inches. "And like *this*. . ." She did it again, until Jack could almost see behind her chair. "What can you see?"

Jack leaned over sideways as far as he could and tried to twist his head down as far as it would go.

Aunt Thea clattered forward again. And Jack

caught his breath. Sticking into the back leg of
her chair, its sharp point embedded in the wood,
was Ninjataur's ninjato sword.

# Chapter 9

# Tricks and Tauronia

Lewis got the spare key out from under Tibbles, the dog-shaped rock in Aunt Thea's front garden, and let Clint into the house. The man grabbed his arm and quickly pulled Lewis in after him, glancing around to see if any neighbours were about in the twilight. Nobody was.

Lewis was pleased. He didn't *want* any neighbours to see anything suspicious. He had plans . . . and they did not include visits from the police or nosy Mrs Peebles from up the road.

"Right, you start searching! I want all those pictures! Now!" growled Clint, flicking the hallway light on.

"We can split up if you like," chirruped Lewis.

"I'll do upstairs and you can do downstairs. . ."

"Not on your life. What do you think I am – an idiot?" demanded Clint, grabbing a fistful of Lewis's hair and tugging his head sideways.

Lewis chose not to say.

Clint dragged him into Aunt Thea's front room, but could see at once that it was neat and tidy and not strewn with abandoned drawings as he'd been led to believe.

"Oh," said Lewis. "Aunt Thea must have had a tidy up. I think she will have put the pictures back in our folder in the kitchen." He'd lied, of course, about the pictures being scattered all around the house and garden. If he'd been truthful and said they were all in a folder in a drawer, Clint could have come and got them by himself without any help. And that wouldn't do at all. Lewis led the way into the kitchen, Clint muttering close behind him, and went straight to the shallow drawer in the large dining table where the folder was kept. He pulled it out and laid it on the table. He slid some of the drawings from it and spread them across the scrubbed pine surface. Clint leaned over his shoulder and stared at them.

"You see," said Lewis. "Here's what we draw – Electrotaur and Slashermite – they're our best friends in Tauronia – and Lavataur and Stinkermite and Grippakillataur and Krushataur (well, he's dead – he fell into a chasm of molten custard)."

"Yeah, yeah," said Clint. "Kid's scribbles. I get it."

"But look – recognize *him?*" Lewis held up the picture of Ninjataur. He felt a pang of sorrow. Poor Ninjataur. He wouldn't have known anything about it, of course, but it was still rather sad that he'd had to explode.

Clint gulped. He realized that this *was* the creature which had held him at knifepoint and spun the boss around like a frisbee. He could see that many of the other pictures were even more gory and fearsome than Ninjataur. But – they *were* only pictures, he reassured himself. Nothing to be afraid of.

"Right, so where's this mead?" he demanded.

"Like I said – it's here, dried into the paper," said Lewis. "I think if you wet it, some of the

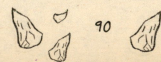

magic in the mead might still work."

"You're not wetting *that!*" Clint jabbed a finger at the picture of Gripperkillataur. "Or that!" He jabbed at Electrotaur.

"No, I won't mead any Taurs or Mites," agreed Lewis. Now he pulled out a picture of the standing stone in Aunt Thea's back garden. On the picture were the words GATEWAY TO TAURONIA – half in Jack's handwriting and half in Lewis's. They had drawn and meaded this picture together because it was important that they both had control over it. Each of them was the master of each Taur or Mite they drew and meaded to life. Although they could persuade each other's creations to do things, they only had *real* power over their own creations – so it was important that they shared power over the Gateway to Tauronia, in case of emergencies.

And this was most definitely an emergency.

"Look," said Lewis. "See out of the window – right at the end of the garden? That's Aunt Thea's standing stone, like in this picture, and we use it as the way out of Tauronia. I can

 91

wet this picture a bit and see if the mead will reactivate. If it does, the gateway will open. That's all. Nothing will come out unless I mead it to come out, so we'll be quite safe."

Clint looked at him doubtfully.

"It's the only way to be sure," said Lewis. "Your boss will be much happier if you can tell him that it works . . . without bringing a monster to life."

"All right," grunted Clint. "Do it."

Lewis filled an egg cup with water from the tap and then spilled a few drops on the drawing. He sniffed it. Yes – he could just about smell the rich honey scent of the mead. He really didn't know if this would work. He had just wanted to try – and even if it didn't work he might have some hope of escaping and going for help while he was alone with Clint.

But if it *did* work. . .

"OK," he said. "We have to go up the garden and see."

Clint stayed close behind him as they walked up past the hedges and through the willow arch to the far end of the garden. It was nearly dark now; the sky was turning violet and the trees and shrubs were in black silhouette against it. The standing stone loomed above them, and then there was a click and a golden light shone on to the bushes behind it.

"Yes!" said Lewis. "See!" He waved the picture under Clint's nose. "This is how it's meant to look. See, a door open in the rock, with stone steps leading down and golden light shining up."

They stepped around the stone to see and there it was. The door was open and the light was shining and the steps were leading away down into the ground.

Clint gaped at it. He looked at the picture in his hand and then back at the gateway. Then he narrowed his eyes at Lewis. "How do I know this hasn't been 'ere all along?" he said. "Who's to say there's anyfink magic about this? It's just a door and a light, innit?"

Lewis looked grave. He nodded. "You're right," he said. "The only way to be sure is to go down a few steps, so you can see."

Clint twitched.

"Unless you're too nervous," added Lewis, quickly. "I mean, it's been a very scary day for you. *I* would be nervous."

"Geddartaway!" Clint shoved him sideways and strode into the stone arch of the gateway, ducking a little to fit in. Then he reached back and grabbed hold of Lewis's wrist and pulled him in too. Clint stomped down the stone steps and Lewis followed, grinning. The steps wound round and down several times, until it was hard to guess how far down they had travelled. Clint didn't seem to notice that there were no electric lights in the rock to account for the golden glow.

At last they reached the bottom step and the whole of Tauronia lay spread out before them. Clint's mouth fell open as if his jaw had been suddenly unhinged. He dropped Lewis's wrist.

A wide valley of green, gold, red and purple landscape wound away from them, surrounded by mountains and volcanoes. A river ran along the bottom of the valley, fed by tumbling waterfalls from the mountainsides which were dotted with castles, near and far. Several small villages were scattered along the bottom of the valley which ended, far away in the distance, at the golden sands beside the glorious turquoise Tauronian Sea.

To the west, just visible on the horizon, were the glaciers and snow fields of the Tauronian Tundra, where Floatingfrostataur lived, keeping the temperature nice and frosty, and to the east there were bubbling red and orange lakes sending up spicy fumes – the Molten Swamps of Badcurry. The wind must be coming from that direction today, thought Lewis. The last time he was here, it was from the north west and he'd smelled the sugary scent of the Candyfloss Fields of Doom.

Taur and Mites of all shapes and sizes wandered the land, but it was hard to make out who was who at a distance. Dragomites flew overhead, chasing small sparkling flocks of Aviamites. A white pebbly path led away from them and wound down towards the town square of Tauronia, where a collection of odd, wonky houses and shops (Jack and Lewis were a bit impatient when it came to buildings which weren't castles) were grouped around a brown statue of two small figures. Creatures of many colours bustled around among the houses and shops.

"I – I – I. . ." gasped Clint, looking as if he might faint. Especially as Millipedataur had chosen that moment to go steaming past on his track, his thousands of legs rippling impressively, carrying an assortment of very weird creatures, on their way from the mountains to the seaside, on his shiny burgundy back. As Clint's eyes widened and widened Scoffataur suddenly opened his huge mouth and ate a Jellymite which had unwisely sat in front of him – whole. Then a giant wobbly orange thing behind him slapped his back and he belched the Jellymite up again, looking sheepish.

"You show him, Blomonjataur!" called Lewis, cheerily, as Millipedataur trundled on. Blomonjataur gave his creator a little wave and then smacked Scoffataur – who was really just a big pink dribbly mouth and a big belly on legs – on the head.

"I – I – I. . ." went on Clint.

"Isn't it brill?" asked Lewis.

"I want to go now," whimpered Clint. "I have to take you back."

"Sure!" grinned Lewis. "You can take me. As

soon as you've caught me!"

And he bolted down the white pebbly path with a whoop, leaving Clint staring after him in horror.

# Chapter 10

# Hug of Death

"Gearly gere!" gurgled Jack, leaning so far forward he thought his chair would tip at any second – and that could be disastrous. Once again he got his teeth around the handle of the late Ninjataur's ninjato sword and clamped them tight before pulling back with all his might.

"Go on, Jack! You can do it!" encouraged Aunt Thea, in a low voice. She had spent some minutes making her chair jump forward, centimetre by centimetre, while Jack had worked his own chair sideways until he was far enough behind her to go for the sword, which must have been flung out into the chair when Ninjataur exploded. "I know you can!" added Aunt Thea. A second later there was a *thhhhuck!* and at last

99

the sword came away from the leg of the chair. Jack rocked back with the recoil and for a few terrible seconds he teetered, swaying, on the back two legs of the chair. If he fell over backwards they would be done for. Even if he managed to keep the ninjato clutched between his teeth after his head had cracked against the stone floor, he would never be able to get himself up again.

He held his breath, willing himself to tip up the right way again and straining forward with all his strength. Clunk! His two front chair legs reconnected with the floor and Jack let out a long, shaky sigh of relief, which whistled around the metal sword in his teeth. Right. Now. He leaned forward again, but this time he didn't need to go so far. Tilting his head to the right he only had to reach Aunt Thea's tightly bound wrists, which she was pulling up from the chair, as high as she could behind her back, so that he could reach the taut rope. In fact it was more like thick string, wound round and around. If he could just saw through one bit of string, the rest would unravel.

"Come on, Jack – I know you can do it!" said

Aunt Thea, trying to glance back at him over her shoulder. Now he was in the right position to cut. He just had to keep his jaws clamped tight and not let the sword slip. He drove the blade carefully against the string and waggled his head back and forth, sawing into it and trying very hard, also, not to slash his aunt's wrists. It was not going to be easy. In fact it might well turn out to be impossible.

But Jack had reckoned without Lewis's creative flair for weaponry in Tauronia. Of *course* the blade would work! Lewis had decreed that it would cut through iron! A bit of thick string was no problem. The string frayed, pinged once and then split apart. Jack sat up again, astonished, while Aunt Thea began to work her wrists free.

*Well drawn, Lew!* he thought. *Well drawn!*

Lewis knew this was insanely dangerous. He was running through Tauronia, alone and defenceless, with no protection at all – unless you counted the Tauronia folder of pictures stuffed down his jumper. He wasn't remotely worried about Clint – just the hundreds of

 101

horrifying dangers that he and his brother had created with crayons and paper. Most of the creatures here could kill you as soon as look at you – if they fancied it. He ought to be safe from any of his own Taurs or Mites . . . probably . . . (in truth, some of the bigger, nastier ones were so big and nasty they might not really care if they snacked on their own creator). Jack's creations, though, could eat him quite cheerfully. Or fry him with a hard stare. Or nip his head off absent-mindedly with a giant claw.

But at least Lewis knew what to expect. He and Jack usually worked on their drawings together, at Aunt Thea's kitchen table, and enjoyed sharing all the details of their creations' powers and weaknesses and quests. In fact, given how murderous they often were, it surprised Lewis to see that Tauronia seemed to be rolling on fairly happily whenever he and Jack had popped down for an emergency reason. All kinds of mashing, charring, head-popping and eating of each other must go on among the monsters here, but somehow they seemed to survive it.

Lewis skirted the Tauronia town square and noticed that the chocolate statue of himself and his brother had been mended. A few months back someone had bitten off his ear, both his and Jack's noses and Jack's elbow. Lewis grinned. Slashermite must have mended the statues. They looked, and smelled, as good as new. A few Taurs and Mites were wandering around, and some of them were staring at him. Lewis scanned the crowd for Slashermite. That's who he wanted to see – or maybe Electrotaur. He glanced up and saw the wildly running figure of Clint, heading down the hillside in pursuit of him. Even from here, he could tell the man was terrified. He was hunched over, running low to the ground, his arms over his head, trying not to look around him.

Lewis giggled. He could see a creature sprinting straight down the slope towards Clint, at an angle. Clint had no idea that it was coming. Not looking around was a very dangerous idea in Tauronia.

The creature pelted across the grassy slopes and threw itself at Clint. It knocked him off his

feet. Lewis giggled some more as the screams began. It wasn't that he didn't care if Clint got squelched – even though he probably deserved it – it was just the look on the man's face as he rolled over and stared up at the furry green thing which was bearing down on him. Cuddlemite swept the man's shocked body into his fluffy arms and squeezed him with great affection. All Cuddlemite wanted was to cuddle the world to rights. A big hug was all that was needed to make everything right again, in Cuddlemite's small, furry brain. If he sensed distress he went in for a cuddle like a heat-seeking missile. And of course, the more distressed you got, the more he cuddled. Tighter and tighter, until you either cheered up or suffocated.

Of course, Clint was very lucky he hadn't been spotted by Grippakillataur. *His* kind of cuddle involved being squished in giant metal car-crusher type jaws in a matter of seconds. But the man was still in danger with Cuddlemite. If he didn't stop screaming and cheer up soon he would very likely be cuddled to death, and Lewis didn't really want that. He ran back up the hill

to where the Mite and the man were grappling together. By now Clint was squawking and beating feebly against Cuddlemite's tight grasp, his face almost totally engulfed in well-meaning fur. Cuddlemite was crooning soothingly at him, but it wasn't working. Clint was totally freaking out – and that could mean the end of him. With every muffled screech, Cuddlemite squeezed a little harder and Clint's arms and legs flapped more frenziedly.

"Clint!" called Lewis. "You have to calm down and start smiling." He could try to get Cuddlemite to stop, but Jack had created this Mite and it probably wouldn't do any good. He was a very stupid creature, too, however kind hearted he was. He wouldn't understand.

An anguished, muffled bellow squeezed out through Cuddlemite's armpit. Lewis reached in among the warm furry embrace and grabbed Clint's ear.

"Listen!" he yelled. "This is Cuddlemite. He cuddles stressed people to make them feel better. If you don't start feeling better and relax he'll just keep on cuddling until you relax anyway. By being DEAD! You *have* to stop fighting and screaming. Calm down and try to smile and he'll let you go."

Clint stopped screaming and his arms and legs flopped down suddenly. Lewis gulped. Maybe he was dead already.

"There, you've made him feel better," he smiled at Cuddlemite, patting the creature's shoulder. "Well done! You can let him go now."

Cuddlemite turned his large round pink eyes on Lewis and beamed a goofy smile. "All better

now?" he asked.

"Yes, he's all better now," said Lewis. "Can you let him go a bit?"

Cuddlemite loosened his hug and Clint came slithering out of the creature's fluffy clutches, looking dazed and semi-conscious. Lewis knelt next to the man and poked his shoulder. "Come on," he whispered. "Smile and say thank you – or there'll be more cuddling."

Clint opened his eyes and stared at Lewis. Slowly he produced a rather panicky smile.

"Good," coaxed Lewis. "Good – a bit more now. Then say thank you, Cuddlemite."

Clint's smile got a little wider and slightly less panicky. He directed it at the monster which was crouching over him wearing a loving expression of concern.

"Th-thank you, C-cuddlemite," he whispered.

"All better now?" beamed Cuddlemite, patting Clint's head with a giant fluffy paw.

"Yeah, yeah, all better now."

"Well done, Cuddlemite," said Lewis. "But can you stay with us? Just in case Clint gets upset again?"

107

Cuddlemite nodded happily, as Lewis grabbed Clint's arm and pulled him up, and the monster flumped along behind them, humming cheerily, as they began to walk.

"Just remember," Lewis said, in a low, warning voice. "You try to grab me or anything, and Cuddlemite will have you! I won't stop him next time."

Clint nodded. He looked white and shocked and was staring around in appalled wonder. "W-where are you taking me?" he whimpered.

"I thought you might like to meet a friend of mine. He'll look after you for a while."

Lewis led Clint through the town square where his bearded ginger jaw fell open in astonishment as assorted Taurs and Mites wandered around staring back at him curiously, suspiciously or hungrily.

Dragotaur was sitting up on one of the wonky roofs, gently fanning her huge leathery wings and blinking her four jewel-like eyes in the rising heat from Lavataur, who was reclining on a pile of large stones, turning them red as his molten rock body dripped across them. Several

Mites were holding marshmallows on sticks out towards him and roasting them. Lavataur winked a blue eye and grinned at Lewis, lazily waving one of his pumice stone clawed hands.

"Hi, Lavi," called Lewis, waving back, and ducking as a small storm of pretty, colourful Aviamites shot past them, squeaking. "Hi, Slashertaur!" he added, as a large, rather clunky Taur with stubby wings and not terribly well-drawn features strolled by, chatting with Tryangletaur, who was walking in a very angular way on his three legs. "Seen your son anywhere?"

Slashertaur froze and stared at Lewis. "Why?" he said. "What does he want? I told him . . . I've nothing more to give!" The Taur started to gulp and sniff. He was a rather emotional character and not a great dad, Lewis had to admit. He wished Jack had drawn him better, with more backbone, mostly, for Slashermite's sake.

"Don't worry," he sighed, but Slashertaur was already rising up, his little wings beating frantically, looking edgily left and right, not wanting to be pinned down to any kind of commitment.

Lewis strode more purposefully, leading Clint and Cuddlemite towards a small shop with a window filled with colourful, sparkly things, under a sign which read: Stinkermite Style – Frocks & Frills For Every Occasion.

He sent Cuddlemite on his way and then flung open the door and called in. "Hey! Stinkermite! Do us a favour. Look after this bloke for a while, will you? Don't let him out until I come back, or something will eat him."

A small, greeny-blue, furry, eyebally creature, wearing a white tutu and diamond-studded wellingtons, emerged from behind the shop counter. He grinned at Clint. Clint's knees went and he sunk to the floor. Then Stinkermite sniffed. Suddenly and hard. His four eyeballs shot out on stalks and the fur on his body began to rotate, making him look a bit like one of those swirly brushy things in a car wash. "Questy, Questy!" he gurgled. "Must chase guff!"

"No!" said Lewis, firmly. "He's just been squeezed nearly to death by Cuddlemite. He needs a break." He looked down at Clint and chuckled. "But you can get him to model some

110

frocks for you if you like. . ."

Clint was staring, horror-struck, at the large lacy lemon ballgown which Stinkermite was getting off a rack, as Lewis left the shop. Lewis checked his watch and gulped. It was six forty-five p.m. He had to hurry if he was going to get Electrotaur and Slashermite and then collect Clint and make him drive them all back to Trindle Castle. If he was late, Jack and Aunt Thea would be no more than two squished worms stuck to Lord Merrion's boot. . .

# Chapter 11

# Ups and Downs

"Blow this! I can't wait!" said Lord Merrion, as he stomped back down into the dungeon, holding several pieces of paper. "If what you say is true, this will make my dream come true all in a matter of minutes! I will have created my destiny! See! Here it all is!" He shook the bits of paper in front of Aunt Thea's nose and she held her hands tightly behind her back, pretending they were still tied.

Jack's hands were also behind his back – because they *were* still tied. Aunt Thea had been just about to get up and cut his bonds too, when Lord Merrion returned. The ninjato sword lay behind her chair, where it had dropped from Jack's teeth, fortunately out of sight. Their

112

captor didn't seem to notice that Aunt Thea's chair had moved forward.

On the bits of paper in his hand were many scribbly drawings in lurid colours.

"What have you drawn?" said Aunt Thea. "A snakes' tea party?"

"It is my theme park!" snapped the lord, flapping the drawings at her, tetchily. "Can't you see that? Trindle Castle Towers! It's obvious – *here* – this is the Tower Toppler – a vertical plunge machine which makes everyone think they're going to plummet head first into the moat, and this is the Castle Corkscrew, the see-through helter-skelter slide in the north turret, and here's the Dungeon Death Train which takes you through the torture chambers where animated lifelike mannequins re-enact famous scenes of inhuman evil, and here's the high speed history tour rollercoaster – the Hysterical Historical. It goes up and down and upside down and through a glass tunnel around the moat and then up one hundred feet higher than the tallest tower and then plunging down, down, down through the dungeons, just missing

the Dungeon Death Train by inches – all with an accurate running commentary of the castle's illustrious history! Oh, imagine the screams! Imagine . . . oh now what?" He was cut off in full flow by another chirrup from his pocket, and got his mobile phone out again.

"What do you want now, Barri?" he huffed. "No! No, I told you – you can't come! It's my castle and you're not allowed in unless I say so! Go back to your own castle."

He snapped his phone shut and went back to marvelling at his pictures. Then he looked at his watch. "Your brother is taking his time," he said, raising an eyebrow at Jack. "Maybe he *wants* you to get turned into a worm and stamped on!"

"He'll be here," said Jack. He tried to imagine where Lewis was right now. Driving back in the van with Clint most likely . . . or . . . or maybe . . . NO! He wouldn't! Would he? Jack had a sudden vision of Lewis running through Tauronia, laughing his head off as Clint stumbled along behind him. It was so vivid that as soon as he'd thought of it Jack became absolutely certain that this was what Lewis had

meant to do, when he went off with Clint. If he *had* managed to reactivate the dried mead by wetting the drawings, he would have got the Gateway to Tauronia open – taken Clint up to see it "as proof", and then somehow escaped into Tauronia. Jack knew this – because it's exactly what *he* would have done.

But if Lewis *had* managed to get away and run off in Tauronia he wasn't much safer. Tauronia was horrifically dangerous. And what if Clint was waiting for him to come out of the gateway? Lewis would be trapped down there. Jack eyed the bottles of mead in the little box as Lord Merrion waffled on and on about his theme park to a weary-looking Aunt Thea. If only Merrion would just push off again then Aunt Thea could undo Jack's tied hands and he could grab some mead and paper and a crayon and draw Lewis another exit – not the spare one in Aunt Thea's rose bush (that was too close to where Clint might be waiting), but one that came out right by Trindle Castle. Even right *in* it – up on the battlements or in the keep or something.

Lord Merrion, though, was not leaving.

"Well?" he demanded, waving his pictures in the air. "Is it not genius?"

"It's nauseating!" said Aunt Thea. "If you had one drop of true noble blood in your veins you would never even *think* of such a thing. The very stones of this castle are shrieking with horror at such a revolting idea. If the walls could talk, there'd be some pretty ripe language here right now! But anyway, you'll never be allowed to have it. The local planning office will make you tear it down in less than a week. To say nothing of the heritage people – and the villagers! They love this place just the way it is. They don't want it turning into a giant plastic funfair."

"The local planning office can't stop me!" he grinned. "Nor can those idiots at the heritage office! Nobody can. Let them try – when I have *this*!" He turned to the box of mead and took up a bottle, uncorked it and—

"NO!" cried Aunt Thea. "It's terribly dangerous! You don't know what you're dealing with here!"

"This, madam, is my birthright!" He held the bottle over his drawings and began to tip it.

"No! Stop! Please!" Aunt Thea could bear it no longer. She threw herself across the room and knocked the bottle out of Lord Merrion's hand. It flew up into the air, leaving a small arc of droplets suspended for a millisecond before they all fell – unfortunately right across the sheaf of wildly coloured drawings in his hands.

"Ha!" he cackled, grabbing Aunt Thea by her hair. "Ha! You can't deny me my destiny! You see? It is meant to be! Wayne! Wayne! Get down here!"

Wayne ran down the steps and wrestled Aunt Thea back to her chair while a warm, eerie wind began to suck through the room. Jack shivered. He knew what this meant. Some big Merrion's Mead magic was happening in the real world. The first time the standing stone had become the Gateway to Tauronia the same odd wind had whipped up.

Suddenly a blast of gaudy light shot down the steps, along with the smell of cheap cooking fat and onions. Lord Merrion squeaked with excitement and then ran upstairs, whooping. "It's here! It's here!" he yelled. "My rides! My

 117

plasma screens! My burger bars! I've done it! I've DONE it!"

Aunt Thea and Jack exchanged appalled glances. And then, while Wayne paused to stare up the steps in wonder, Aunt Thea leaped to her feet and did the most impressive Kung Fu style kick Jack had ever seen. The heel of her best green leather boot cracked into the back of Wayne's head and he fell over like a sack of potatoes. Seconds later, Jack was freed and running for the rest of the mead. He grabbed the bottles and shoved them deep into his jeans pockets and then snatched up a spare bit of paper and a pencil.

"We've got to run!" hissed Aunt Thea, checking Wayne, who lay dribbling on the floor, but didn't look too badly hurt. "Quick! While Lord Merrion is distracted by whatever is up there!"

"No! Not yet! We need more help! And so does Lew." Jack drew quickly and with great concentration. The first side of the paper was for Lewis's exit from Tauronia – the second was for something quite different.

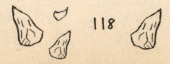

118

As soon as he was finished and had dropped mead on the drawings and the writing that went with them, Jack joined Aunt Thea in running up the steps. What they saw as they emerged into the castle courtyard took their breath away.

The whole scene was brilliantly lit with thousands of lights, of all colours, many pulsing on and off, reflecting back from a shining plastic fairyland of kiosks, flickering plasma screens, chocolate vending machines, burger bars reeking of fat and overcooked onions, a popcorn fountain, a "Guillotine Yourself" game with an instant photo booth attached to it, a swooping rollercoaster skimming a few feet above their heads, blowing their hair up like a fan, and maniacally spinning, waltzing, dodging and whirring rides in all directions. High energy music pumped out of myriads of speakers set around the stone walls while a small amusement arcade revolved slowly on a giant golden sovereign and little electronic carts rolled around offering large mallow lollipops shaped to look like the severed heads of traitors on spikes.

It was the most ghastly sight Aunt Thea had ever laid eyes on. She quite forgot to grab Jack's hand and run, but stood rooted to the spot, gaping in horrified disbelief.

A throne of carved gold, set with rubies, emeralds and diamonds, suddenly rose up in the air on a hydraulic lift. In it sat Lord Merrion, wearing a crown and a fur-lined golden robe. "You see!" he bellowed down at them, too excited to notice they had escaped. "You see! This is my destiny!" His chair flickered slightly,

and Aunt Thea and Jack could see the stone walls through it for a fraction of a second. They glanced at each other.

"NOW! Before I turn you into worms – you will ride! You will ride my magic mead rides! You will have the honour of being my first passengers!" declared the lord. His throne descended and he stepped down from it and strode towards them, his robe rising in the updraught of all the wildly gyrating machines.

"Not on your life!" said Aunt Thea, grabbing

Jack's hand, but as she did so she felt fingers go around her throat. Wayne had woken up. His head hurt and he was not in a good mood. "Jack! Run!" she yelled, but Jack did not.

"Go!" chortled Lord Merrion. "And never see your aunt again."

Jack folded his arms. He had no intention of leaving now. Not even if he *and* Aunt Thea were free to go.

"To the Hysterical Historical!" cried Lord Merrion, waving his arms around like a demented windmill and running towards the alighting station for the rollercoaster. The glistening new machine glided slowly along slender golden rails, coming to a halt by the Aluner just as he got there. It seemed to be made of some kind of blue crystal, with silver bar things that clamped down over your chest to keep you in place. It had little heraldic shields engraved along its sides, and red satin cushions on its seats. Sleek black headphones hung from the headrests and Aunt Thea and Jack could already hear the tinny running commentary coming from them.

"On! On!" yelled Lord Merrion, giving his crown to Wayne to hold. "We will ride! We will all ride!" He was so excited that he was spitting again, sending a gobby shower all over the nice shiny sides of his creation.

Again, Jack noticed the whole thing flicker, like a mirage, but it felt completely solid when he cautiously put his hand out to touch it. The flickering hadn't escaped Aunt Thea either. "We can't get on it," she said. "It's not safe."

"Nonsense!" scoffed Lord Merrion. "It's the safest ride in the world. *I* made it! Do you think I would dream up something unsafe which could wreck my new business by squashing a customer? Now stop being such a girl and get on!"

Aunt Thea sighed. "You're too old to use Merrion's Mead," she said. "That's why this is unsafe. I have made things too, you know, with the mead. They are unreliable because I am too old to believe in them *properly*."

"Well I believe in THIS!" snapped the lord. "So shut up and get on or it's worm time for you." And from his jacket pocket he pulled a drawing of two stick-like figures turning into worms. He hooked a bottle of mead out of his other pocket and waved it menacingly near the picture.

Aunt Thea got on and Jack got into the same car and sat next to her. Lord Merrion put his bottle and picture back in his pockets and chose the seat in front so he could turn back and stare at them excitedly. "Put them on! Put them *on!*" he commanded and they put the headphones on, to hear a plummy female voice say: ". . .at the turn of the fifteenth century. She was also to lose her head after displeasing the king with her poor embroidery skills – and her skull is buried in the churchyard of. . ."

"Fantastic, isn't it?" panted Lord Merrion, spraying them with more excited spit and nodding to Wayne to push the START button as he stood beside the ride. "It's that posh bird off the telly, you know, who was in *The New Revengers* and does those insurance adverts. I got her for free! In fact. . ." his eyes went dreamy. . . "I might get her here and imprison her in the south tower . . . in a nice long dress. Yes! That

would be an attraction and no mistake. Joanna Plumley . . . actress in residence. . ."

There was a lurch and the ride suddenly sped forward at tremendous speed, knocking the breath out of all of them. "In 1544 the castle was besieged by plague victims," Joanna Plumley quickly informed them. "They were incensed that Lord and Lady Trindle had Aluncaded themselves in and were doing nothing to help their people. The villagers took revenge by flinging some of their dead across the battlements by use of a trebuchet, to infect the nobility. . ."

They shot suddenly skywards, like a rocket, and everyone screamed – even Lord Merrion. The ride threw them towards the stars and then suddenly arched over with a stomach squelching whoosh and sent them plummeting face first back down towards the battlements.

". . .this is how it must have felt for the hapless plague victim on the trebuchet. . ." went on Joanna. "Had he or she still been alive. . ."

# Chapter 12

# Awkward Angles

"Stinkermite!" Lewis stood at the door, flanked by Electrotaur and Slashermite, and stared crossly at his unruly four-eyed Mite.

"Honestly! I leave him in your care for *ten* minutes and look what's happened!"

Clint sniffed miserably in a triangular sort of way. He was not having a good day.

"But master, he would not try on the purple strapless!" sulked Stinkermite, holding out a bejewelled sparkly gown. "He became upset. He ran from the boutique and I could not stop him before he met Tryangletaur."

Lewis sighed. That much was obvious. Clint was not wearing a frilly Stinkermite Style outfit,

as Lewis had expected. Instead he was a perfect equilateral triangle. His whole body – and the clothes on it – had dramatically changed shape, so that his head was stretched wide, both ears reaching up into the points of exact sixty degree angles, while his chest and lower body were now tapered into the third angle at the bottom. His eyes, nose and mouth looked tiny in the middle of all the weirdly stretched skin. His arms and legs sprouted awkwardly from his odd new torso. There were still a couple of Tryangletaur's little triangular arrow-heads stuck in his trouser legs.

All Taurs and Mites had quests – and Tryangletaur's was to turn things into triangles. He felt compelled, at least once or twice a week, to try to "correct" the shape of something by firing his triangle points at it. You couldn't blame him. And after all, he believed that he had *improved* Clint.

This was a view that Clint did not share. He was sniffling loudly. "Get me out of here," he whimpered, through his tautly stretched ginger beard. "I'm sorry I was mean to you. I'll never

 127

be mean again. Just get me out of here and back to normal."

Lewis looked at his watch and then at Slashermite, his small, purple, rhino-horned best friend in Tauronia. Slashermite scraped his long blade-like fingers together anxiously and nodded at Lewis. "We are running out of time, master," he agreed.

"WE MUST GO," boomed Electrotaur, who stood back from the doorway a little as he was eight foot tall and couldn't fit under it easily. He was a magnificent golden-scaled Taur, created and meaded by Jack, with fingers shaped like lightning and a non-stop buzz of electricity about him. His magnificence was only slightly diminished by wearing what appeared to be a pair of Rupert Bear style trousers, which Jack really ought to get around to redrawing. Electrotaur could send bolts of lightning from those fingers, while the end of his tail and his intense green eyes frequently sent off little showers of sparks when he was agitated. They were sparking a lot right now. Electrotaur knew his master was in danger and he was desperate to save him.

128

"Yes, we must go," agreed Lewis, eyeing Clint. "But I think we're going to have to take him along – because only Jack can undo the triangle thing. Can you carry him, Leccy? He'll slow us down otherwise."

"I CAN," said Electrotaur. "TURN ME DOWN."

Lewis nodded and reached across to the purple dial in the middle of Electrotaur's chest and turned it down to about three. This was the safety device Jack had added because Electrotaur sometimes got too highly charged and became dangerous to touch. He could give you a nasty shock, but with his dial turned down low he was fairly safe.

Clint squeaked with terror as Electrotaur leaned over, picked him up and clasped him over one shoulder like a toddler.

"It's all right," said Lewis. "He won't hurt you. Probably."

They set off quickly towards the path which led back up the hill to the exit to the Overworld, Electrotaur marching sturdily with the triangular Clint grimacing over his scaly golden shoulder and Slashermite bouncing

along and scraping his finger-blades together in excitement and worry. Slashermite was a very caring Mite in spite of his fearsome appearance and he loved Jack and Aunt Thea almost as much as he loved Lewis.

Lewis kept an eye out all the time for trouble. He knew Tryangletaur might try to "improve" *him* into a perfect triangle at any moment – although the Taur was nowhere to be seen. Lewis thought Clint would still be able to drive the van, even with his bizarre new shape. He just hoped they would make it back in time. Surely Lord Merrion wouldn't *really* turn Jack and Aunt Thea into worms . . . would he? Lewis shook his head and tried not to think about it as they climbed the hill. He needed to stay focused. They would get to the castle and Electrotaur and Slashermite would help him to rescue Jack and Aunt Thea.

There was a rumble under Lewis's feet. At first he didn't pay it much attention. There were several volcanoes in Tauronia, and they could go off at any time, although they were never really that destructive. Some of them just

belched out hot frogs. Then there was another rumble. And a familiar sweet smell.

"Oh no!" yelled Lewis. "The Custardreas Fault! It's breaking open again! Quick, everyone, in here!"

He dragged Slashermite into a nearby cave in the hillside (there were many useful caves and tunnels riddling this world) and Electrotaur thundered in behind them with Clint, seconds before a vast avalanche of hot yellow custard blew past the cave entrance and on down the hill. For a minute or two they sat quietly, waiting for the hot steam off the custard, now coating the hillside around them, to drift away as the yellow blanket cooled. At last Lewis looked out and surveyed the view further up the hill. A dense curtain of steam, two or three miles long, billowed up high into the air. The Custardreas Fault ran wide and deep.

"It's no good," he said. "The chasm will be open for at least an hour. It takes that long to close up again. We can't get to the gateway. We'll have to use the second exit, the one Aunt Thea made for us last time we got trapped. Jack redrew it afterwards, so it should still work. It should open up in the plinth of our chocolate statue and come out in Aunt Thea's rose bush.

They began to run back down the hill. Lewis was sweating and shaking. He reckoned there was less than fifteen minutes now before Lord Merrion turned Jack and Aunt Thea into worms. He was too late! Even if they got out without further delay, there was no way he could get them all back in time. He was a rubbish rescuer. Could things possibly have gone worse?

At that moment, things got worse.

A spinning cloud of flying custard globules should have warned Lewis – but he was still shocked speechless when out of the yellow storm of pudding sauce careered the terrifying, hungry, ruthless shape of Toastataur.

"AAAAAAAAAAAAAHHHHHHHH!" screamed Jack, Aunt Thea and Lord Merrion.

The Hysterical Historical had just swung them all upside down and downside up, under

and over in a hideous corkscrew, and now it was about to splat them into the thick stone wall of the outer keep. A fraction of a second before they were all strawberry jam, the wall transformed into a dark tunnel and the rollercoaster whooshed inside it, displacing a great big chunk of air and making their ears pop with the pressure.

Another fraction of a second and they were under water. Bubbles and weeds and surprised-looking fish suddenly bloomed around their heads, lit by ghostly underwater lamps. The Hysterical Historical was hurtling through a round glass tube which seemed to be circling the castle, submerged in the moat.

"A few hundred years ago you would not have seen fish swimming through the waters of this moat as you can today," revealed Joanna Plumley, in her posh velvety voice. "But you would see plenty of poos. The castle toilets, or garderobes, were emptied directly into the moat. . ."

Jack saw the tunnel around them do another little flicker and he felt a few drops of water

 133

strike his face. He hoped (really) these were just more gobbets of spit from their drooly host – but he was terribly afraid, even beyond being terribly afraid *anyway*, that they were drops of moat water. This ride was unstable – as unstable as poor Aunt Thea's Invisitaur and her personal Hero on Horseback, who had been given to leaving his limbs lying around in the back garden. Both had only vaguely existed and couldn't really be relied upon for anything. Grown-up creations with Merrion's Mead just seemed not to last. They had realized that this was probably because no matter how much a grown-up *wanted* to believe in magical stuff, they just couldn't fully do it. That power seemed to belong only to children.

*Swoosh-CLANG!* *Swoosh-CLANG!* Now they were soaring up again, at a forty-five degree angle, past a line-up of huge metal axes – the kind used to chop heads off – and between every gap of every car on the ride, the axes were swinging down, positioned to skim past the terrified noses of the passengers, miraculously missing any of the workings of the

rollercoaster and any human flesh. Jack had to admit, grudgingly and through a big wave of travel-sickness, that Lord Merrion certainly did know how to design a rollercoaster. It was amazing – but then, it had been created by magic, which had to help.

The ride had now moved into a series of stomach-churning zig-zag moves and at every zig-zag point of the rails they were travelling, they were lurched forward as if they were about to come off the track. Finally the car slowed down and climbed slowly up, up, up, until it seemed to be hanging in space, with the castle courtyard far below.

As Jack stared in horror at the hideous drop, so sheer that he was unable to see any kind of track at all, Aunt Thea squeezed his hand in hers and yelled, "Nearly over!" Below, Jack could make out the dizzying array of whirling and waltzing rides with their multicoloured lights. And he thought he saw another man walk into the castle courtyard. Maybe Clint was back with Lewis – but this man looked taller and darker than Clint as he

stared around in amazement.

Jack had no time to wonder any more, though. At that moment he was pitched forward and the ride began to plunge to the courtyard so fast that he felt his lips and cheeks billow out like a parachute. This was surely going to kill them all.

## Chapter 13

# Lording It

Death. For at least one of them. Lewis couldn't see any way out in the seconds they had before Toastataur struck. Electrotaur was carrying Clint and Slashermite was too small to help. By the time Clint had been dropped and Electrotaur had powered up and thrown a bolt of electricity at the fire belching beast, it would be upon them. Toastataur had been designed by Jack only a few weeks ago. He had eight metallic legs and a spider-like body, and his head was a huge flared nozzle of rusting iron, with two mean orange eyes on high antennae above it. From the mouth of the nozzle, Toastataur could throw out a powerful jet of flame and incinerate anything in about three seconds. He ate pretty much anything, sucking his food up through the same hole – but first it had to be toasted until it was just a pile of black chunks.

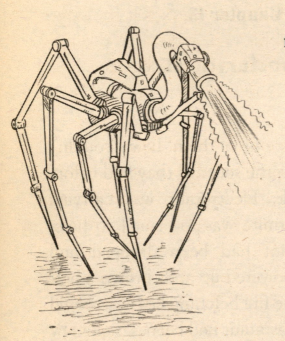

A rumbling sound issued from Toastataur's body. The furnace inside him was powering up. His orange eyes stared at Lewis, hungrily. Lewis was the closest. This was certainly the end and at least he could say it had never been boring! It would probably be quick too. "Bye, Slashy," he sighed, closing his eyes. "Bye, Leccy." He felt a warm tingling sensation around his neck. It should get a lot hotter any second now.

Electrotaur tried to dump Clint on the floor but the panicky triangle of a man squealed and hung on like a limpet. However scary Electrotaur was, Toastataur was pant-wettingly horrific.

As Toastataur flung forward his nozzle head and prepared to blast fire, Lewis felt the tingle again. He opened his eyes and stared down in amazement at the orange button set into a large medallion on a chain around his neck. There were words on it: EMERGENCY EXIT.

He lost no time wondering about where it had come from. He pressed the button. There was a sudden punch in the air around them all. It blew Toastataur backwards into the custard, his eight legs waving in a frenzy. Billowing out in front of Lewis's amazed face, was a bright red, self-inflating door – in its own doorframe. In two seconds it was standing upright and firm on the hillside. The words EMERGENCY EXIT glowed in white neon tubing on the front of it and the round door handle was flashing blue, like the lights of a fire engine.

Lewis lost no time in whacking it open. With a whoop he dragged Slashermite through. Electrotaur and Clint followed. The moment

the door closed behind them, it folded up into nothing and then disappeared with a small chime.

The castle courtyard flew up to meet them and this time Jack was certain they would be pulped. It felt as if the car they were in was in freefall.

But, as the unforgiving ground zoomed towards Jack's face, the ride did an abrupt loop upwards and they found themselves gliding along gently to the alighting platform. All three of them lay back in their seats, looking like shocked fish.

Eventually Jack said, "WOW!" He couldn't help it. It was the most terrifying, amazing, mind-blowing ride he'd ever been on. He didn't like rollercoasters at all, but he knew people who did, who would have been whooping with the thrill of it.

Lord Merrion staggered out of his seat and grinned proudly at them. And then threw up on his shoes.

Jack and Aunt Thea got hastily out of

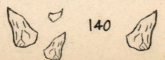

the car and on to the platform beside the ride, where Wayne stood, folding his arms and blocking their escape. Behind him and beyond the dazzling lights of the other rides and attractions, the dark wall of the inner keep seemed to flicker and shift. A waft of mossy, earthy air reached Jack's nose and he smiled.

"And now," said Lord Merrion, wiping his mouth with a grubby handkerchief and looking at his watch, "I think it is worm time."

Jack and Aunt Thea tried to run but Wayne grabbed Jack, and Aunt Thea could not leave without him. "It's all right! Run!" he yelled, but she wouldn't leave him.

The lord had his worm drawing out and was now rummaging through his pockets for the mead, grinning maliciously. "You see!" he chortled. "You see! I am master of my destiny! Lord of all I have created! I allowed you the ride of your life – and now I will give you the ride of death! For I AM LORD MERRION!"

"Oh no you're not, boyo," said a deep voice behind them. Aunt Thea turned and stared.

And *stared.* Standing well over six foot tall, his dark hair swept back from a high, noble forehead, piercing silver grey eyes dancing in the glitter of a thousand fairy lights, and shoulders broad and strong in a long dark coat, stood a strange man.

Lord Merrion froze, gaped and then looked thunderously angry.

"I think you'll find," the man said icily, "that I am Lord Merrion."

Lord Merrion – the first one – pursed his lips

and looked very sulky. Then he stamped his foot. "Just because you're the oldest! Doesn't mean you should have the title! It's not fair!"

Aunt Thea gaped from one man to the other. "Is this your brother?" she asked the new Lord Merrion.

"Sadly, yes, madam," he replied. "Please allow me to introduce myself – I am Lord Barri Brynley Drystan Merrion, knight of the garter – and here to assure you that *nobody* is going to get turned into a worm while *I* am here!" He gave her a stiff bow, looking her directly in the eyes and allowing an amused smile to hover about his well-chiselled mouth.

"Oh," said Aunt Thea, suddenly terribly aware of what the Hysterical Historical had done to her hair.

"Ha!" cackled the Lord Merrion who apparently wasn't Lord Merrion. "That's what *you* think!" And he rummaged again for the mead.

"Looking for this?" said the real Lord Merrion, holding up a twiggy wooden bottle. "It must have dropped out of your pocket while

you were looping the loop in that devilish contraption. What have you done to my castle, Alun? You were meant to get it restored – not turn it into Disneyland From Hell!"

"It's not your castle – it's mine! Mine, I tell you!" stropped Alun. "You said to come here and take over the rebuilding and that's what I did – but I did much better than that! Much better! I am going to make it a success! A phenomenal success beyond your wildest imaginings, Barri! Much, much better than your boring old pile of rocks up in the Valleys. My castle is never going to be a boring old pile of rocks again! Look at it! Just look at what I have created! Trindle Castle Towers!" He glanced over at Wayne. "Quickly – get me the rest of the mead!"

Wayne edged backwards with Jack still trapped in his arms, unaware that the remaining two mead bottles were now in Jack's jeans pockets (despite the ride), along with a folded piece of paper with a drawing on both sides. One drawing was the Emergency Door for Lewis – the other was a Taur. A

Taur made of rocks.

Wayne stopped. Suddenly. He had to. There was a solid rock wall behind him. And the solid rock wall was getting up on its feet. The solid rock wall was angry. Very angry indeed. As Wayne turned round, astonished, and stared up, his eyes round with disbelief, Jack whooped with delight.

At last. ROCKATAUR had arrived.

## Chapter 14

# Between a Rock and a High Place

Everyone drew in a sharp breath as they took in the full magnificence of Jack's creation. Standing half as high as the castle battlements, Rockataur was made entirely of rocks from Trindle Castle – from the pile out by the front gate, in fact; the rocks that had been retrieved after rolling down the hillside over centuries and were due to be restored into the old walls. Now they had a more urgent purpose.

Rockataur had boulder-shaped muscles on his arms and legs, a portcullis across his mouth, which made him look like he was grinning in a very alarming way, and two golden eyes below crenellated brows, which were burning with fury at Alun Merrion.

"You!" bellowed Rockataur, in a deep, grating voice. "You despoil me!"

The fake Lord Merrion opened his mouth but nothing came out except a small mewing noise. Standing at the Taur's immense block-like feet, Wayne frantically rubbed his earlobe and then gave up the fight and just fainted.

"You!" went on Rockataur, sweeping a huge granite fist through the air, scattering old soil and lichen, and thumping it down on the ground. "You turn this place of beauty into a tawdry circus! You seek to profit from the destruction of history and heritage! You are a traitor to your name!"

"Couldn't have put it better myself," said Lord Merrion (the real one), standing next to Aunt Thea and taking the whole staggering scenario really quite calmly, she thought.

"This castle has a punishment for traitors," Rockataur boomed on. "Ready your head, sir, for a spike above the gate!"

"Well, I wouldn't go *that* far," added the real Lord Merrion.

Alun staggered backwards, up on to the platform of the Historical Hysterical.

147

"Prepare to meet your ancestors!" bellowed Rockataur, flexing his stone fingers with a grating noise, ready to grab the traitor by the head.

Then there was a doorbell chime and a blast of custard scented air, and out of nowhere jumped Lewis, Slashermite, Electrotaur and a triangle on legs. Everyone turned and gasped again, and as they did so there was a whooshing noise and Alun shot away on the Hysterical Historical, one hundred feet out of reach of Rockataur.

"Ha!" he shouted down at them as the rollercoaster looped over and made its first descent. "You'll never catch MEEEEEEE!" Beneath him the car he was riding in flickered, and the silhouette of the north tower could clearly be seen through it. Aunt Thea shut her eyes.

"Oh no," she said. "It's not going to last. It's going to fall apart at any second now."

"What do you mean?" asked the real Lord Merrion.

"He's magicked all this into being with Merrion's Mead!" She opened her eyes and stared up, shaking her head. "But Merrion's Mead

doesn't work properly unless it's been used by a child!" She blinked as Alun shot past, screaming, "IIIII'LLGEEEEEETTTTYOUUUUUUU!" and disappeared through the castle wall before Rockataur could snatch him out of his seat.

"I know – I've tried it myself," went on Aunt Thea. "All my creations are dodgy and insubstantial and they always fall apart in the end. See the way all these rides are fading?" They looked around and saw that she was right. The rides and stalls and the rotating amusement arcade were either fading out or flickering or pixellating like a bad signal on satellite TV. The Hysterical Historical was no different. Random parts of its tracks were crumbling away into nothingness. By the sound of it, Alun was just passing through the falling axes now, and would soon be shooting up to the high zig-zag part of the track. Except that this part was now mostly zig and hardly any zag.

"Oh my word. He's going to fall," murmured Lord Merrion as the blue crystal cars shot back into view, high, high above the castle on the

149

dwindling track.

"Good thing too!" said Lewis, coming to join them. "Who's *he?*" he asked Aunt Thea.

"The real Lord Merrion," she said, staring up at the unfolding calamity above. "What's that triangle thing?"

"The unreal Clint," said Lewis. "Had a run in with Tryangletaur."

"Look, I know Alun's a low-down kind of character and I wouldn't trust him as far as I could fling him," said Lord Merrion. "But he *is* still my brother. I have to try to save him." And he ran to the foot of the ride — what was left of it — and tried to climb up and shout a warning.

"Jack!" called Aunt Thea. "Quickly! You have to get Rockataur to help, or Alun up there is going to be Merrion marmalade!"

"Rockataur doesn't want to help him!" pointed out Jack. "He wants to pound him into the flagstones. And remember — that's what Alun was going to do to us! Under his boot!"

"Now is not the time for revenge, Jack," said Aunt Thea. "Tell Rockataur to be ready. He's the only one who can save him."

Jack ran to Rockataur and climbed up his left leg, calling out instructions. The reluctant grating noises in response did not sound encouraging. Lord Merrion abandoned his attempt to scale the ride – there was nothing left to climb at ground level – and stood back, watching, with sad distress upon his noble face.

As all of the rides began to conk out, the musical cacophony also subsided until all they could hear was the swooping and rattling of the rollercoaster and Alun shouting out, "You'll never stop meeeeeeeeeee!" high up above them.

Then his car hit the zig, discovered there was no zag, and shot out into thin air.

"It's my destineeee-eeee-eeee-eeee-eeeek!" screamed Alun, hurtling down in a wild spiral as the rollercoaster undid itself behind him and began to snap out of reality, chunk by chunk. Soon only Alun himself remained, plummeting towards the ground, his arms and legs flailing wildly.

Rockataur scooped a fistful of moss from a

nearby wall and held out his giant granite palm. A second later there was a *doof* as the creator of Trindle Castle Towers – such as it now was – landed in the mossy cushion in Rockataur's palm. His stone fingers closed together, not crushing Alun, but forming an immovable cage.

"Aaaaaaaaaaaaw," came a wail from behind a rock thumb. "My theme park! My beautiful,

beautiful theme park . . . it's all gone! It's not FAIR!"

It was true. Trindle Castle once again looked like Trindle Castle. All the rides and kiosks and plasma screens and burger bars were gone. A single marshmallow traitor's head on a stick floated in a puddle, slowly dissolving.

There was a long pause.

Then Clint said, "Can someone *please* un-triangle me?"

# Chapter 15

# Tea for Two

"Earl Grey?" asked Lord Merrion. "Or perhaps Lady Grey?"

"Lady Grey would be lovely," said Aunt Thea.

"I prefer that myself," said the lord. "Much more delicate flavour. Hobnob?"

"I'd better not," sighed Aunt Thea.

"You should. After all you've been through a Hobnob is entirely called for." He put several oat biscuits on a china plate and added this to a silver tray, containing a teapot, cups and saucers and a little jug of milk. He placed the tray on the polished oak table by Aunt Thea's armchair and pulled up a footstool for himself. The fire blazed in the hearth, sending a warm

glow across his handsome features as he poured the tea, and highlighting his noble cheekbones to perfection.

If only she could block out two gurning boys, a purple, blade-fingered monster, itching to shred a priceless tapestry, an eight foot electricity beast staring hungrily at the plug sockets, a sobbing minor noble trapped in a stone hand outside the diamond-paned window and a man begging not to be a triangle, it would really be quite romantic.

"Oh do stop staring and get on with sorting out Clint," she told Jack. Jack got back to the business in hand and meaded his quick sketch of Tryangletaur. A few seconds later his creation was standing on the wine-coloured rug.

"No you don't!" said Jack, as soon as Tryangletaur reached for his bag of triangle points, which he could flick like mini frisbees at anyone he wanted to turn triangular. Tryangletaur paused and looked put out. "You have to un-triangle him now," said Jack, pointing at Clint. "You know what to do."

Looking very sulky indeed, Tryangletaur

rummaged around in the green felt bag and drew out a couple of circles. They looked like large tiddlywinks. With very little enthusiasm,  the Taur flipped them through the air to land on Clint. There was a hissing noise and the sixty degree angles of Clint's body began to soften into curves. A few seconds later the hissing stopped and Clint was his normal shape again. He sobbed with relief until Aunt Thea gave him a cup of tea and a Hobnob, just to shut him up. Wayne had no such luxury. He was currently

156

imprisoned in Rockataur's other hand, still barely conscious. Rockataur sat out in the courtyard, too big to come inside, and glanced through the windows from time to time.

Jack sent Tryangletaur back to Tauronia with a splash of mead and then joined in with the tea and biscuits, along with Lewis.

"So, how long have you had the mead, Miss Casterbridge?" asked Lord Merrion in his rather charming Welsh voice.

"Oh, for nearly a year now," said Aunt Thea. "And do call me Thea."

"Only if you call me Barri."

Lewis looked at Jack across the rug and made a retching face.

"Don't," muttered Jack. "It won't last long. In half an hour he'll be hypnotized to forget all this, along with the others, and he'll never remember he was chatting up Aunt Thea."

Lewis nodded across at Slashermite. It was very fortunate that Slashermite could hypnotize anyone to forget anything or believe anything or do anything – as long as Lewis told him to.

Without Slashermite, several people in their town, who went about leading happy normal lives, would be gibbering wrecks.

As they drank their tea and ate their biscuits, exhausted and thrilled with how it had all turned out, Aunt Thea told Lord Merrion the whole story of how she had found the mead and brought it home, and given it to Jack and Lewis. How their monster drawings were accidentally meaded to life, and all the adventures they had since been through, finishing with this latest one.

"I cannot apologize enough for my brother," said Lord Merrion. "He has always been terribly jealous of me. Being first born, I inherit the title and the castles – but in fact they are all held in trust for the nation and for all of our children and grandchildren. I feel it is my life's work to restore and preserve them – and I tried to encourage my brother to do the same by putting him in charge of Trindle. But Alun has always had other ideas. He always wanted to be rich. He heard about the legend of Merrion's Mead when we were children and became obsessed

with it. Of course, I didn't really believe in it until today, but Alun always imagined it could be real and that one day he would find it and make himself rich."

"But surely your family *is* rich," said Aunt Thea. "You're a lord! A knight!"

"Yes . . . but only rich in old castles," laughed Lord Merrion. "Not cash! It doesn't matter to me, but it does matter to Alun. He wants to be a singing star, don't you know? To record albums and fill the Albert Hall."

Aunt Thea grimaced.

"Ah. I see you have heard the Merrion Male Voice Choir," nodded Lord Merrion. "Sadly, singing is not one of my brother's talents."

"I'll tell you what he *is* talented at," said Jack. Everyone looked at him in surprise. "Making rollercoasters," he said. "No – really. It was horrifying! But amazing. I reckon he should go into theme park design – that's what I reckon."

"But without magic to help him, eh?" smiled the lord. "Shame about that. I wouldn't have minded a little magic myself. Are you sure it won't work for me?"

"Not reliably," said Aunt Thea. "Which is worse than not at all. As you saw. I wonder how old the original Lord Merrion was when he first tried it."

"Oh, that's easy," said Lord Merrion, sipping some tea. "He was thirteen."

"Thirteen?" echoed Aunt Thea and Jack and Lewis, surprised.

"Yes, Owain became Lord at the age of nine. Got his mead made to celebrate becoming a man at thirteen. Died in the Merrion castle moat at sixteen, just after he had married Gwen. She had her baby son a few months after she was widowed – my great great great great grandfather. So, if he hadn't been chased into the moat by the giant pillow or whatever it was, I'm guessing Owain's meading powers would have faded soon anyway. You can't really be a child any more once you're a father."

"I suppose you're going to make us give the mead back now," said Lewis. "Your birthright and all that."

"Not at all. Your aunt paid for it – it's yours."

160

Aunt Thea dabbed at her eyes. "You really are quite perfect, Barri," she sniffed, waving at Lewis and Slashermite. "I don't know if I'm ever going to be able to get over this."

"Get over what?" he smiled, and there were wonderful little crinkles at the corners of his eyes as Slashermite began waving to him.

"Look," sniffed Aunt Thea. "Slashermite wants to show you something. . ."

## Chapter 16

# Mead's End

The kitchen sink gurgled. Tap water ran across the stainless steel and curved itself around the plughole, draining away in a small whirlpool. Aunt Thea held up a twiggy bottle and began to tip it over.

"Please don't," sniffed Lewis.

"Please don't," gulped Jack.

Aunt Thea sighed and set the bottle back down on the draining board. She turned to face her nephews with a resolute expression on her face. All through breakfast she had explained what they must do – but obviously she must explain it once again.

"Jack – Lewis. Please try to understand. Merrion's Mead has been wonderful. But I

cannot allow this to go on. Just *think* about all the disasters that we've had to deal with! Monsters running amok in the Overworld – people getting nearly crushed or eaten alive. Your whole school getting possessed and buried under killer finger-knitting! And a perfectly lovely castle being turned into a revolting money-making theme park – to say nothing of all of us nearly getting turned into worms and squished."

"But what about all the *good* things!" argued Jack. "Electrotaur and Slashermite saving your garden and the standing stone from getting demolished and built over! Cousin Timmy learning to eat proper food and stop guffing at people all the time. Your friend being able to save her farm because of Spacemite pretending to be a visiting alien in the sky over her field."

Lewis bit his lip and did his best big eyes. "If you tip away the mead and burn all the pictures, we'll never see Electrotaur and Slashermite again."

Aunt Thea took a deep breath. "But they won't be destroyed. They will go on living

and running around in Tauronia the same as before. Spacemite will still pop up into the sky above Carol's field every few weeks and keep all the UFO hunters coming and buying stuff at her farm shop and café. All the things you've created will go on living."

"But we'll never see them," said Jack.

"And you'll never get eaten by them, either," said Aunt Thea. She was still shuddering after hearing how close Lewis came to being barbecued by Toastataur. "Boys, I know you love your friends from Tauronia. I love them too. But if I keep letting you play with the mead, one day something terrible will happen and I will never be able to forgive myself. I know we've done some amazing things, but I can't help thinking that we've done some pretty awful things too.

"After all, none of that business with Trindle Castle would have happened if you hadn't been shouting about Merrion's Mead, Lewis. I'm sorry, but it's true. Nothing much good has come of all that, has it? I still can't get that ear shredding Merrion Male Voice Choir CD out

of my brain." She smacked her brow twice and then shook her head ruefully.

"No, it was just a lot of messy horror, for us and for those men, then they all got hypnotized to forget. Nobody learned anything. Nothing good happened."

"We made Rockataur!" said Jack, smiling winningly. "He was brilliant. And now he's building his own perfect Trindle Castle down in Tauronia. He said we could go and visit it when it's done. . ." Jack trailed off as his aunt glared at him.

"Exactly," she said.

"You met a bloke you fancied," giggled Lewis.

Aunt Thea huffed and folded her arms. "Yes, Lewis. I did. I met quite possibly *the perfect man*. Only problem was, we had to HYPNOTIZE HIM TO FORGET ME! Remember?"

The phone rang as Lewis opened his mouth to reply. Aunt Thea strode across the room and snatched up the receiver. "Yes?" she snapped. Then her eyes widened and her mouth formed a little "o" of shock. "Oh . . . oh . . . hello. Yes.

Yes we did." She made a "what the heck?" face at Lewis and he ran across and hit the speaker button, so they could hear who was on the line.

"I'm very glad I was able to find your phone number," rang out a cultured Welsh voice with a distinctly lordly tone to it. "I found it in my coat pocket on a scrap of paper and remembered how lovely it was to meet you at Trindle Castle yesterday. I hope you don't mind me calling."

"Well, no, of course not, Lord Merrion," gasped Aunt Thea, still staring questioningly from Lewis to Jack. "But . . . er . . . what do you remember about our meeting, I wonder. . .?"

"Well, we happened to bump into each other up on the battlements, while you were there with your nephews, and I was talking to my brother, Alun, and we fell into a most riveting conversation. And I felt we really hit it off."

"We did?" murmured Aunt Thea, going rather pink. "I . . . I mean, yes, we did."

"So, I wondered if you would be interested in coming to visit my other castle – Merrion Castle, in Wales," went on Lord Merrion. "Some time next week, perhaps? I would send the Rolls Royce to collect you, of course. You would be very welcome to stay for a few days if you can spare the time. I would love to hear about your work as a travel writer and all the places you've been to, and perhaps you would be interested in the history of the Merrion family . . . do you know, it's even got its own magical legend?"

Aunt Thea smiled. "I would be delighted,"

she said. "Um . . . will your brother be there, by any chance?"

"What, Alun? Oh no. He won't, as you ask. Funnily enough, he's *just* been in to see me this morning at Trindle Castle – we both stayed here last night – and he's told me the most extraordinary thing."

Everyone gulped.

"He said he's going to university! Tomorrow! Can you believe it? He's going to university to do film, animation, engineering and business studies. Told me he's going to set up a business designing rollercoasters from now on. Can you believe it? At forty-four? Well, good for him, I say. I don't mind looking after Trindle Castle, in his place. It's lovely, even though it needs some work."

"Yes, a bit more restoration yet," agreed Aunt Thea, still pink and smiling but now narrowing her eyes suspiciously at her nephews. She realized that Lewis and Jack must have put Slashermite up to some fairly complicated hypnosis to make all of this happen. Probably while she was on her third Hobnob, gazing into

Lord Merrion's perfect silver grey eyes.

"Yes, do you know, we've had some rock go missing? Since yesterday! There was a huge pile of rocks out the front, ready for restoration work, and overnight they vanished. As if they just got up and walked away!"

Lewis and Jack burst into laughter. The rocks *had* got up and walked away.

"Ah well, never mind," the lord was saying. "We'll find plenty more down the hillside. And I'm so delighted you can come to visit. I'll ask the car to call for you at ten a.m. on Tuesday. . .?"

"Please do – I'm very much looking forward to it." Aunt Thea replaced the receiver and patted her hair.

"Soo-ooo," said Jack. "Still think nothing good ever comes of Merrion's Mead?"

They all looked at the three bottles on the draining board. Two full and one half full.

"Well," said Aunt Thea. "We should at least find a better hiding place for them. . ."

169

**Look out for the other
Monster Makers adventures**

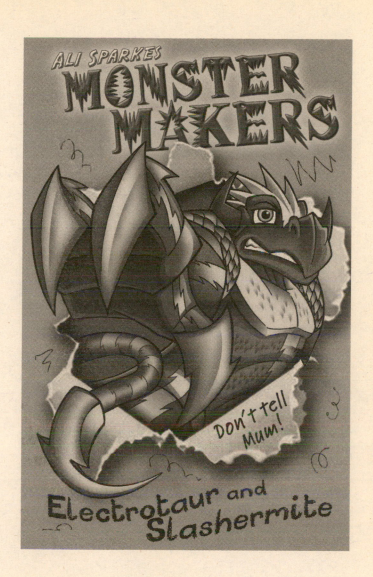